Bu

Cozy Mystery Series Book 25

Hope Callaghan

hopecallaghan.com
Copyright © 2025
All rights reserved.

Visit my website for new releases and special offers: hopecallaghan.com

CONTENTS

Cast of Characters

Carlita Garlucci-Taylor. The widow of a mafia "made" man, Carlita promised her husband on his deathbed to get their sons out of the "family" business, so she moves from New York to the historic city of Savannah, Georgia. But escaping the "family" isn't as easy as she hoped it would be, and trouble follows Carlita to her new home.

Mercedes Garlucci. Carlita's daughter and the first to move to Savannah with her mother. As a writer, Mercedes has a knack for finding mysteries and adventure and dragging her mother along for the ride.

Vincent Garlucci, Jr. Carlita's oldest son and a younger version of his father, Vinnie, is deeply entrenched in the "family" business and not interested in leaving New Jersey for the Deep South.

Tony Garlucci. Carlita's middle son and the second to follow his mother to Savannah. Tony is protective of both his mother and his sister, which is a good thing since the female Garluccis are always in some sort of predicament.

Paulie Garlucci. Carlita's youngest son. Mayor of the small town of Clifton Falls, New York, Paulie never joined the "family" business and is content to live his life with his wife and young children away from a life of crime. His wife, Gina, rules the family household with an iron fist.

Chapter 1

"I hope everything is okay. When I talked to Steve on the phone earlier, he seemed upset." Carlita hustled to keep pace with her daughter, Mercedes. "He was looking forward to the fundraiser, but now he's threatening to call it off."

Steve Winters, a Garlucci family friend and owner of the Shades of Ink tattoo shop, had been struggling financially to keep his doors open and the lights on at his business for several months.

Carlita and a bunch of other Walton Square business owners had come up with a plan to host a fundraiser for him and Paisley, his girlfriend, to raise some much-needed funds, enabling them to get back on their feet.

Mother and daughter reached the shop, where they found the couple waiting inside, both of their faces mirroring a look of defeat.

"Uh-oh." Carlita said the first thing that popped into her head. "Please tell me whatever happened doesn't involve Elvira."

"It has nothing to do with Elvira," Paisley said. "Steve and I know how hard you've been working to plan this fundraiser. We don't want to waste any more of your time and we're thinking maybe we should call it off."

"What makes you think we'll be wasting our time?" Mercedes asked. "I'm positive we can rake in enough dough to get you back in black with enough left over to set aside for a rainy day. This doesn't even factor in the raffle tickets we've already pre-sold."

Steve handed Carlita a piece of paper. At the top was the name of a local investment bank. It was a letter addressed to Shades of Ink. She lowered her gaze and read the subject line aloud, "Notice of Foreclosure."

"The bank is foreclosing on this place?" Mercedes asked. "Their timing is impeccable."

"It's useless. There's no way we can raise enough money to catch up." He took the paper from Carlita and tossed it on the desk. "I'm ready to throw in the towel. Maybe I'm a crappy businessperson, and this is my sign to sell and go get a different job."

Mercedes folded her arms. "You can't quit."

"I'm not quitting. I'm giving up," Steve said. "The worry is eating me alive."

"And keeping us both up at night," Paisley added.

Carlita could hear the stress in both their voices and had no doubt they viewed this as a sign it was time to "pack it in." But they were close...so close to finally digging their way out of their financial hole. She needed to convince them they should hang on a little longer. Hours, literally. "Everything is ready to go. Cool Bones and his band are itching to perform.

The food from Ravello's and the Parrot House Restaurant is being prepped as we speak."

Mercedes picked up. "All the silent auction gifts— and there are a ton—are gonna bring in stacks of cash."

"Mark and Glenda Fox have invited close friends from the Brick District, friends with deep pockets and the spirit of giving," Carlita said. "Not to mention Tori Montgomery has invited quite a few people with money. Mark my words. Not only will this fundraiser get you out of the hole, but it's going to put you over the top."

Steve frowned. "What if you do all of this for us and we still can't get caught up? To me, this foreclosure notice is the icing on the cake."

"We won't know until we try," Carlita said. "Don't deny your friends and neighbors the opportunity to do a good deed and help one of our own."

"Steve and I will feel terrible if you put in all this time and effort and it still doesn't solve our problems," Paisley said.

"Thinking you're somehow wasting our time should not even be a thought in your minds." Carlita patted Paisley's shoulder. "We want to help. Besides, I think we're going to knock it out of the park. You'll be rolling in dough."

"I can only dream of this being the case." Steve placed a light hand on the back of his neck, eyeing them thoughtfully. "Do you really want to host the event, knowing there's a chance it won't turn things around for us?"

"I look at this as a challenge." Carlita tapped the top of the foreclosure notice. "It's even more motivation to get Shades of Ink back on its feet and your money problems behind you."

He looked away, but not before Carlita noticed the tears in his eyes. "You're a big part of Walton Square," she said in a quiet voice. "It wouldn't be the same without you."

5

"Thanks, Carlita, Mercedes." Steve impulsively hugged them. "As long as no matter what happens, we're still friends."

"Friends forever." She hugged him back. "Put the letter in the drawer and know that the next time you pull it out, you can call the number and tell them you have the money to get caught up on your loan."

"While we're here, Ma and I figured we could start unloading the raffle items. They're in the pawn shop's storage room," Mercedes said.

"We can help."

Working as a team, the group of four ran back to Savannah Swag, the Garlucci family's pawn shop, grabbed the auction items and carried them to Steve's place.

He placed the last box on the floor by the door and dusted his hands. "Elvira swung by earlier. She told me she was sorry she would be missing the fundraiser, but wanted to let me know she donated an EC Investigative Services background search."

"She's leaving for Alaska." Carlita glanced at her watch. "Thanks for the reminder. I need to get going. I'm dropping her off at the airport this afternoon."

Paisley wrinkled her nose. "She's gonna go all the way up there to look for gold?"

"Sort of. She's meeting with some gold mining folks to learn the ropes, although something tells me Elvira won't stop at just learning how to goldmine."

"Me either," Steve said. "She'll tear Alaska apart trying to strike it rich."

"We may never see her again," Mercedes said.

"Bite your tongue." An uneasiness settled over Carlita. She'd had several dreams about Elvira recently, all involving her upcoming trip. In them, she'd become involved in some sort of trouble, although Carlita was never quite clear what exactly had happened. Knowing Elvira and her quest for riches, the dream might not be too far off.

Her trip had all the makings of a calamity waiting to happen. When Elvira became laser-focused on a project, she acted impulsively, giving little thought to her safety and the safety of those around her.

Hence, Carlita's concern. Elvira had never stepped foot in Alaska, didn't actually know the people she was meeting and planned to visit a rugged and remote area—a trifecta of factors which seemed like a recipe for disaster.

The only saving grace was the fact her boyfriend Sharky would be "somewhere" in the vicinity, along with Millie Armati, a Garlucci family friend. On the flip side, neither of them knew she was heading their way.

To hear Elvira talk, she had everything under control. After all, she owned a security services company and assured Carlita she would be safety and security conscious. Still, the trip concerned her, and she couldn't shake the ominous feeling something bad was going to happen.

After leaving Steve's shop, mother and daughter parted ways in the alley. Carlita crossed over to her former neighbor's building and knocked on the door. No one answered. She tried again, this time pounding her fist and ringing the bell. Finally, a flustered Elvira appeared. "Hey, Carlita."

"Hey, Elvira." She tapped the top of her watch. "For a minute, I thought you found another ride to the airport. Are you ready to go?"

"Almost. I was wondering if we could take one of the work vans. I already have my gear loaded up."

"Gear?"

"You know…the stuff I'm going to need for mining."

Carlita's eyes widened. "How much stuff are we talking about?"

Elvira began rattling off her list.

She cut her off. "I agree. We should probably take your van."

"Cool. I'll be right out." Elvira slammed the door in her face. She opened it moments later, fully dressed and raring to go.

Carlita burst out laughing.

"What's so funny?"

"This." She flipped the flap of the plaid hat perched atop Elvira's head. "Where on earth did you get this?"

"Online." Her brows knitted. "It's a genuine trapper's hat. Believe me, it's going to come in handy in the blustery arctic weather."

"Arctic weather? As in...you're expecting it to snow?" Carlita had a hard time believing there was a chance of snow falling in September.

"No, but hey, the forties and fifties are cold, especially to warm weather people like us."

Elvira had a point. The temperature difference would be noticeable, especially for a southerner who was accustomed to the mild Georgia climate. Plus, if it made her happy to dress like a trapper...who was she to rain on her parade? More power to her.

"It's a good look." Carlita fell into step, trekking down the alley to the parking lot. "When are you coming back?"

"In a couple of weeks. I plan to hang out with the gold-mining production crew and then hop on board Siren of the Seas, if all goes well," Elvira said.

"Meaning, if Sharky doesn't freak out about you showing up unexpectedly?"

"Something along those lines." Elvira muttered under her breath, and Carlita let it drop. Clearly, the woman had a plan. Whether her boyfriend would be on board could be an entirely different story.

Elvira tossed the keys to her and climbed into the passenger seat. "Before I forget, Dernice said she'll let you know if she needs someone to keep an eye on Snitch. She seems to think she'll be okay."

"But if she starts to show signs of distress, she's more than welcome to hang out with Gunner," Carlita offered.

"Thanks. She said she would keep it in mind."

During the ride to the airport, Carlita kept the conversation light, asking questions about Elvira's itinerary. Unfortunately, the more she asked, the more her concern grew. The woman's plan was to wing it, basically traveling by the seat of her pants.

Her only concrete arrangement was to meet with the gold mining team to work for a couple of days as an apprentice before making her way to Whittier, where she would wait for Siren of the Seas to dock and surprise Sharky. None of which sounded like a good idea. But then…it was Elvira, a woman who was anything but conventional.

"This might be a dumb question, but do you have enough money to pay for your trip, for travel expenses, stuff like that?"

"Yeah. I have some cash and a few credit cards, although I don't foresee using them much. I mean, I only need a few days' hotel stay. Plus, the film crew offered to let me bunk in their travel trailer. I'm not sure if I'll take them up on it. I'm not much into communal living."

"Particularly with people you've never met," Carlita said.

"They seem like decent folks, but you never know. I got a couple of ideas and am leaving my options on the table," Elvira said. "My main goal is to learn as much as I can about mining, maybe strike out on my own for a day or two and then hop on Sharky's ship to enjoy a little R&R with my babe."

"I hope it all works out," Carlita said. "Call me if you need help or if something comes up."

"Will do. I was gonna bring Dernice's lucky rabbit's foot but I forgot."

Keeping her eyes on the road, Carlita unzipped her purse. She reached inside and pulled out one of her restaurant's monogrammed ink pens. Mercedes had convinced her mother to hang onto it, insisting it was good luck after she used it to scratch off a winning lottery ticket. "You can borrow Mercedes' lucky pen."

Elvira's eyes lit. "Is this the one she used on the five hundred dollar scratch-off ticket last week?"

"It is." Carlita held it out. "Maybe it will bring you luck, too."

"Thanks." Elvira took it from her and tucked it in her coat pocket. "I see the unloading area for Alaska Airlines."

"I see it too." Carlita eased the van alongside the curb. She hopped out and caught up with Elvira near the side door, watching as she unloaded her checked bag, a carry-on and finally her bulging backpack. "I think this is everything."

"Are you sure you're ready for this big adventure?"

She gave her a thumbs up. "As ready as I'm ever gonna be. If I have my way, I'll be a whole lot richer the next time you see me."

"Safe travels."

"Thanks." With the ear flaps of her trapper's hat flapping in the wind, Elvira dragged her bags through the open gate. She turned once and gave Carlita a jaunty wave before disappearing from sight.

"Good luck, my friend," she whispered under her breath. "Something tells me you're gonna need it."

Chapter 2

"I'll take care of the balloon display." Mercedes gathered up the bouquet of balloons, leaving Carlita to figure out the configuration of the tables displaying the raffle items.

Steve, noticing her dilemma, came to her rescue and brought over a third table. They arranged the trio in a U-shape, which helped spread out the display.

A sense of accomplishment and pride washed over Carlita as she stood back to inspect their handiwork. So many of the Walton Square business owners and friends had stepped up to help Steve and Paisley get back on their feet.

Autumn had even convinced the head honchos at the Channel Eleven News station to give her some precious airtime to pimp the upcoming party and fundraiser to their local viewers, enticing them with all the goodies being raffled off—and there were a bunch.

Carlita pulled the list from her pocket and double checked to make sure the numbers matched the items up for raffle.

-Sam Ivey: Downtown tour—Group of 4
-Colby's Corner Store (Ken Colby): Gift basket, valued at $200.
-Elvira / EC Investigative Services: A background search with follow-up consultation.
-Savannah Swag Pawn Shop: Gold necklace, valued at $500.
-The Parrot House: 2 dinners.
-The Flying Gunner: 2 tickets for the pirate show.
-Ravello's Italian Eatery: Catered dinner for 2 at the winner's chosen location.
-Mercedes Garlucci: Author signed hardcover book of choice.
-Autumn Winter: Picnic gift basket: wine, cheese, goodies.

-Cool Bones: Entertainment gig / package, for a three hour Cool Bones and Jazz Band concert.

The list went on, with other area businesses who donated goods and services—a pub crawl, haunted ghost tours, spa packages, everything Savannah and then some.

After confirming the tickets matched the prizes, she logged onto her iPad to go over the extensive RSVP list. Shades of Ink would be wall-to-wall people, all opening their pocketbooks to help one of their own who was in need.

Carlita finished her checklist only moments before the food arrived. There were plates, platters, bowls and trays of Italian dishes from Ravello's, along with a tantalizing array of pub fare from the Parrot House Restaurant. Cool Bones and his band arrived and began setting up near the reception area.

It was all hands on deck with Pete, Tony, Mercedes, Paisley, Steve, and Carlita directing workers and gearing up for the big night.

At precisely six thirty, the guests arrived. Steve stood near the door of his tattoo shop, thanking them for coming. With serving staff from Ravello's and Pete's restaurant on hand to help with the food, the party progressed seamlessly. Food, drinks, dancing, and catching up with friends and neighbors.

Breaking away from hosting, Carlita lingered off to the side, taking it all in. It warmed her heart to know the locals had come out to pitch in and make the event a resounding success, not only by purchasing raffle tickets but also donating at the door.

Mercedes caught her mother's eye and made her way over. "At the risk of patting myself on the back, I think it's safe to say we knocked this party out of the park."

"We did. Thanks to a lot of hard work and Autumn, along with Channel 11 News, helping us reach as many people as possible."

"Speaking of Autumn, I think she's in trouble over by the beverage station."

Carlita followed her daughter's gaze, noticing the young woman was trapped in the corner by a tallish man, on the thin side and with gray hair.

"The guy was hitting on me earlier, commenting about my hair and how nicely my dress fit. He looks like he's getting a little too chummy with Autumn now."

"Let's go rescue her." With a look of determination in her eye, Carlita marched across the room with Mercedes hot on her heels.

As luck would have it, by the time they got there, Mr. "Overly Friendly" had moved on.

"Hey, Mrs. T." Autumn's tense expression relaxed. "It looks like we're running low on cups. Do you know where they are?"

"In the closet." Carlita eased past her, pulled out the box, and set another stack on the table. "Thanks for keeping an eye on the beverages. Who was the guy that just walked away?"

"A local business owner. He recognized me from my show, the one featuring this fundraiser. He wanted to know what it would take to feature a story about his business. I've had a few of the area businesspeople asking me how to get some airtime."

"Because you're a local star now," Carlita teased. "Your Divine Eats in Savannah show has made you famous. I know for a fact you've helped Ravello's attract new customers."

"I thought he was trying to put a move on you," Mercedes said.

Autumn grimaced. "All the while we were talking, he was looking me up and down. He also made a flirty remark about my dress."

"He did the same thing to me, making suggestive comments about how nice my dress hugged my curves in all the right places."

"Now that I think about it, I believe he mentioned owning a car dealership somewhere in Savannah."

"Shame on him for his behavior," Carlita scolded. "He's old enough to be your father. At least he's gone now."

Mercedes bounced on the tips of her toes. "We don't have to worry about him cornering us again. He just walked out the door."

"With a young woman. Maybe he got lucky and picked someone up. I say good riddance." Autumn clapped her hands. "Have you noticed how many raffle tickets are being sold?"

Carlita had been keeping tabs. According to her calculations, they were running low and sold even more than she originally anticipated.

Eager to get a jumpstart on the fundraiser, Colby's Corner Store, Ravello's Italian Eatery, the Garlucci's pawn shop, Pete's restaurant, Elvira's business, along with several of the other local business owners had done some pre-selling at each of their locations. "They're being snapped up left and right."

"Sweet," Autumn whooped. "At this rate, Steve and Paisley will be able to catch up on the mortgage and maybe even get ahead."

"By all accounts, I would be shocked if we didn't raise enough money between the raffle and donations at the door."

Midway through the event, during the band's fifteen-minute break, Steve took the stage. "I want to take a moment to thank you for coming out for our fundraiser. I also want to give a special shout out to Pete and Carlita Taylor, Mercedes Garlucci, and my sister Autumn for all of their hard work in organizing the event." He motioned to the band off to the side. "Last, but not least, I want to thank my good friends, Cool Bones and the Jazz Boys, for the awesome tunes tonight."

Steve paused, and Carlita could see he was becoming emotional, his lower lip trembling. "I'll be the first to admit, I'm a proud man. The thought of holding a fundraiser was the farthest thing from my mind. It's been humbling to admit I...we...need help."

While he talked, Paisley quietly made her way to his side.

"Thank you from the bottom of my heart for showing up, for donating prizes, for your support. This..." He swept his hand in a wide circle. "This is what Walton Square and Savannah are all about. I love you. I appreciate you, and I hope when this is all over Shades of Ink tattoo shop will be around for many years to come."

He set the mic back on the stand, grasped Paisley's hand and stepped off the stage to a thunderous round of applause. The crowd moved aside to let them pass, but not without pats on the arm, slaps on the back, hugs and words of encouragement.

Carlita looked away, sudden tears burning the back of her eyes. Steve was right. It was a humbling yet incredible show of support not only within their small community but also within their beloved city.

The hours flew by, and before she knew it, Mercedes took the stage to announce the winning tickets. One by one, the gifts were claimed and the festivities wound down.

Not long past midnight, only a few stragglers remained, those who offered to hang around and help clean up. The leftover food was boxed and stored in the fridge for Steve and Paisley.

Disassembling the folding tables was quick and easy. Meanwhile, Paisley, Autumn and Dernice, who had been "late to the party," having to cover a security job during her sister's absence, helped remove the decorations while Carlita swept the floor.

Finally, the last remnants of the party were gone. Carlita propped the broom in the corner and limped over to where the others had gathered. "Well? Do we have a final tally of how much we raised?"

"We do." Mercedes triumphantly waved a sheet of paper in the air. "Anyone want to take a wild guess?"

"Two grand," Autumn said.

"More."

"Three thousand," Pete guessed.

"More," Mercedes sing-songed.

"Four plus some change," Carlita said.

Her daughter jabbed her thumb up.

"Five thousand dollars?" Paisley gasped, pressing her hand to her chest.

"Not even close. The fundraiser brought in sixteen thousand, seven hundred and fifty-two dollars," Mercedes said. "Some attendees didn't want raffle tickets. They just wanted to give cash in addition to the donation at the door."

"Which means we made over seventeen thousand dollars if you factor in the pre-event raffle tickets sold."

26

"Yep."

Steve whistled loudly. He lifted Paisley off her feet and spun her around. "Not only are we gonna get caught up on our mortgage, but we'll *also* be able to put some money aside."

Carlita clapped her hands. "This is great news. At the risk of saying I told you so...I told you so."

Steve set Paisley down and wrapped his arms around Carlita in the biggest bear hug she'd ever had. "Thank you. I don't know how I can ever repay you for putting this fundraiser together."

"You're welcome." She hugged him back and held him at arm's length. "I like a happy ending, when the good guys actually get ahead."

Luigi ran over to grab a leftover bottle of champagne. "I propose a toast."

"A toast," Mercedes echoed.

"To the best bunch of business owners in all of Savannah."

"Here. Here." Dernice lifted her glass. "I'll toast for Elvira."

"You helped just as much as she did." Carlita lightly clinked her glass to Dernice's. "Here's to safe travels and big adventures for your sister."

"May she return to Savannah with a bag full of gold," Pete joked.

"Or tales of some whopper adventures," Luigi said.

"It's getting late. I'm beat." Carlita and Pete were the first to head out. "Do you need to swing by Ravello's?" he asked as they stepped outside.

"I texted Arnie earlier. He said there was nothing for us to do." Carlita slipped her arm through Pete's as they meandered along the sidewalk. "I'm thrilled Steve and Paisley will be able to catch up on their mortgage."

"More than catch up." He squeezed her hand. "Thanks to you. With a fresh start, I'm confident it will be smooth sailing from here on out for them."

"You know it."

The couple reached the corner, near the front entrance to Savannah Swag, the Garlucci's pawn shop.

Crunch. She tightened her grip on Pete's arm as her foot slid. "Whoa."

"Careful." He reached out to steady her.

Crunch.

"The sidewalk is slippery." Carlita shifted her foot, noticing shards of broken glass scattered across the sidewalk. "It looks like broken glass."

Her first instinct was to check the pawn shop's front window. Much to her relief, a quick inspection revealed the glass appeared to be intact. "Maybe someone broke a bottle."

Pete stepped back and lifted his gaze. "It wasn't a broken bottle. The window above the pawn shop is busted out."

Chapter 3

Carlita's heart plummeted as she gazed up at the broken window above the pawn shop. "What in the world? That doesn't go anywhere."

"Maybe it was some kids messing around."

"Let's grab a ladder and check it out." Carlita fumbled around inside her purse for the keys to the pawn shop. Adjacent to the business and connected by a lower level hallway was her apartment building. Her tenant, Luigi Baruzzo, lived in the studio unit which shared a common wall with the pawn shop. Four larger apartments were located on the second floor, catty-corner to the family business.

The upper-level busted window didn't access anything. In other words, it was merely a cosmetic facade.

After tracking down a ladder, Pete climbed to the top. Using his cell phone's flashlight, he shined it inside and along the narrow wooden plank that ran the length of the building. It was a small space, barely large enough for a person to crawl through. "Someone was in here."

"I bet when they found out it didn't go anywhere, they were sorely disappointed."

Pete descended the ladder and brushed his hands on his slacks. "I'll call the police to report the incident."

After placing the call and while the couple waited, they checked out the pawn shop. Thankfully, the store hadn't been touched. Carlita suspected whoever broke the window discovered there were surveillance cameras covering every square inch of the property and decided to hightail it out of there.

Within minutes, a patrol officer arrived. A woman, one Carlita thought looked vaguely familiar, appeared. As she drew closer, she realized she had met her during a previous incident. "Officer Jonkers."

"Mrs. Garlucci. I thought I recognized the name when the call came in."

"It's Mrs. Taylor now. Pete and I got married."

"I would like to say it's nice to see you again," Pete said. "Unfortunately, we seem to cross paths with you when we're dealing with unpleasant situations."

"A hazard of the job," she joked. "I got a call about a break-in."

Carlita briefly explained what had happened.

"I'll take a look around." Jonkers inspected the busted window, along with the inside of the pawn shop. After finishing, the trio reviewed the surveillance camera recordings. Not long past ten, two individuals dressed in dark clothing appeared to be casing the joint.

They left the scene, only to return a short time later. At roughly ten-twenty, they threw something toward the side of the building. Seconds later, a shower of broken glass rained down. With a rope in hand, one of them tossed it in the air.

Carlita squinted her eyes. "Can you tell what they're doing?"

"It looks like they have some sort of hook on the end of their rope," Jonkers said.

The smaller of the two burglars tugged on the rope. Leveraging their weight, the figure wearing dark clothing began climbing the side of the building and disappeared from sight. Long seconds ticked past. The burglar eventually reappeared.

Meanwhile, their accomplice stood on the sidewalk, keeping watch.

The burglar who had done the climbing grabbed hold of the building's drainpipe and shimmied down. The person was roughly halfway when the pipe broke off, sending them tumbling.

Recovering quickly, the climber sprang to his feet and limped toward the street. "He broke our drainpipe." Although the lighting was poor, Carlita could see the pair arguing. The "climber" grabbed the rope and shuffled off with his accomplice by his side.

They continued watching the surveillance recording until Carlita and Pete appeared.

"It looks like they thought they were being clever, bypassing the alarm system by sneaking into the upstairs window, only to discover it didn't go anywhere."

"And broke my pipe on the way down." Carlita blew air through thinned lips.

"I'm sure I don't have to tell you that you'll want to get your window fixed as soon as possible." Officer Jonkers spun in a slow circle, surveying the inside of the pawn shop. "What's upstairs?"

"Nothing but an attic. Across from the attic space are apartments." Carlita explained there was a single lower unit and four on the second floor, connected by a hallway and a set of stairs.

"Would it be okay if I chatted with your tenants to see if they heard or saw anything?"

"You can. Unfortunately, we were all attending a fundraiser down the street," Pete said.

The cop stared at him. "So...the whole place was empty when the burglars broke in?"

"Correct. It seems like a pretty odd coincidence," Carlita said.

"Like maybe the burglars somehow knew no one was around," Pete added.

"I wouldn't rule this out as an inside job. How many people were at this fundraiser?" Jonkers asked.

"At least half of Savannah." Carlita told the cop it had been broadcast on a local news channel. "It was a fundraiser for a Walton Square business, Shades of Ink. Almost all the neighbors were there."

"Sounds like a crime of opportunity. I'm sure you're aware pawn shops are attractive targets for thieves—jewelry, guns, collectibles, all stuff worth stealing."

"Which is why we have cameras on every corner." Carlita tapped her chin thoughtfully. "They don't strike me as being professional burglars."

"Most thieves and thugs aren't. They're looking for quick cash or stuff they can sell on the streets." The cop jotted some notes in her notepad, handed them the preliminary police report, and told them to call her if they came across any new information.

Her radio went off, dispatching her to another nearby location. It was Colby's Corner Store.

Carlita's heart skipped a beat. "The owner of Colby's store was also at tonight's fundraiser."

"Looks like your place wasn't the only one on the burglar's radar." Jonkers excused herself. She climbed back into her patrol car and sped off.

Pete turned to Carlita. "This isn't a fluke."

"Nope. Someone knew about the fundraiser, saw their opportunity and targeted us." She tapped her foot on the floor. "I have a bad feeling about this."

"Because you think there could be more?"

"Yep."

Although Officer Jonkers had already walked the perimeter of the buildings, Pete and Carlita made another round, carefully checking for signs of an attempted break-in.

The couple returned to their starting point. "I have to say, I'm sure when they saw all of Elvira's high-tech camera equipment, they decided maybe they should try an easier target."

"I hope you're right. While we're here, we might as well check her building." Pete motioned toward Tony and Shelby's place. "I see the lights are out at Tony and Shelby's."

"I'll wait until tomorrow morning to let Tony know what happened. There's no sense in waking the family up at this late hour." Carlita shoved her hands in her pockets. "If I remember correctly, Dernice is a night owl. She might still be up."

Backtracking, they checked the alley first, making their way to the shared parking lot at the end. With a quick look inside the vehicles, Carlita was relieved none of them had been messed with.

Turning right, they walked along the back of the building before circling around to the front. "Elvira's gadgets and gizmos must have deterred the burglars."

Pete turned his phone's light on and flashed it along the front of her building, focusing it on the upper level. "Hold up. I think I see something."

Carlita followed his gaze. Sure enough, the vent cover was crooked. "Someone was trying to get into the air return vent?"

"And possibly even succeeded." Pete motioned to her. "Do you have Dernice's number handy?"

"I do." Carlita pulled her cell phone from her purse and scrolled through her list of contacts. She sent

Dernice a quick text message, asking if she was home.

Her reply was prompt. *Yeah. I'm here. What's up?*

Carlita: *Pete and I are standing out front. Can you meet us?*

Dernice: *On my way.*

She arrived only moments later, a concerned expression on her face. "What's going on?"

"Burglars busted out the window above the pawn shop," Carlita said.

"The window to nowhere?"

Pete and Carlita took turns filling her in on what had happened. "While Officer Jonkers was writing her report, she got called to Colby's Corner Store."

"Something is going on." Dernice told them she returned from the fundraiser and found the office files scattered around. "I figured it was probably an employee trying to find something and left the place in a mess. Elvira would have had a hissy fit, but seeing how she's gone, I chalked it up to it being an employee who was in a big hurry."

"Or maybe someone was inside."

"The doors were locked. I didn't notice where anyone might have tried to break in."

"Same for the pawn shop. Of course, the burglars didn't get anything because the window they sneaked into doesn't lead to anywhere." Carlita tilted her head, studying the crooked vent cover. "Have you ever noticed the vent cover being off kilter before?"

Dernice stepped in next to her, lifting her gaze. "No, but you're right. It's definitely crooked."

"We should probably check it out." Pete led the way inside. Starting in the front, the trio worked their way back, thoroughly searching the lower level before heading upstairs. "What's up here?"

"Boxes and junk. Elvira keeps talking about someday renovating it and turning it into apartments for extra income."

They reached the upper level, most of which was wide open. It appeared the previous owner had made a half-hearted attempt to finish it and gave up. Hence, stud walls were in place, but there was no drywall.

"Where's the light switch?" Carlita ran her hand along the wall.

"The lights don't work," Dernice said. "There's a short in the wiring. Elvira is too cheap to get it fixed."

Pete took the flashlight Dernice had grabbed on her way up the steps and began checking the rooms. While she waited, Carlita wandered over to the wall facing the street.

Dernice caught up with her. "Are you trying to figure out where the vent comes in?"

"Yeah." Carlita shifted her gaze and studied the ceiling. "I see the ductwork."

Pete appeared. "There's no one here. It doesn't look like anything has been messed with."

"Can I borrow the flashlight?"

"Sure." He handed it to his wife.

Carlita shined the light along the metal ductwork, pausing when she noticed what looked like a sag, caused by the weight of something heavy. "There's a dip in the ductwork."

Dernice darted over to the corner and grabbed a broom. Using the end, she began tapping along the perimeter. She reached the dip. With a little more force, she pushed up.

Pop. The duct popped, echoing loudly in the wide open space.

Carlita stumbled back, clutching her chest. "You scared the daylights out of me."

"Sorry," Dernice apologized.

"I keep thinking someone is gonna come crashing down."

Pete grabbed a baseball bat sitting in the corner.

Dernice finished tapping and pushing, making her way to the vent cover on the side wall. "This is where it ends."

Keeping a firm grip on the bat, Pete used his free hand to flip the latch on the cover.

Carlita reached out to stop him. "What are you doing?"

"Taking a look inside."

Thump. The ductwork, only a few feet from where they stood, made a thumping sound.

Dernice's eyes grew round as saucers. "I hope I'm wrong, but I think there's someone in there."

Chapter 4

Pete signaled for the women to head toward the stairs. "Call 911."

"Already on it." Carlita's finger trembled as she dialed the number, bracing for an intruder to come crashing down.

"911. What's your emergency?"

"Yes. I'm at EC Investigative Services' office. Someone has broken into the building. We think they might be trapped in the ductwork."

"What is the address?"

Carlita rattled off the address and thanked the operator, who promised an officer had been dispatched.

She and Dernice hovered off to the side, watching while Pete began gently tapping on the vent with the tip of his bat.

"Someone needs to go downstairs and wait for the police."

"I'm not leaving you," Carlita stubbornly replied.

"I'll go." Dernice dashed down the steps, reappearing a few minutes later with Officer Jonkers hot on her heels.

"You again. What's going on around this place?"

Carlita explained what had happened, how after Jonkers left, they walked around the neighborhood and noticed Elvira's vent cover was crooked.

"We keep hearing noises inside the ductwork," Pete said.

The cop reached for her radio and called for backup.

"I'll run back downstairs to let them in." Dernice took off again.

While they waited, Jonkers told Carlita and Pete she'd left Colby's Corner Store. "Based on the description and surveillance recordings, it appears the same individuals who broke your pawn shop window broke into the store."

"Did they steal anything?"

"Food and supplements."

"Supplements?" Carlita wrinkled her nose.

"Vitamins and protein drinks. I have to admit, it's an odd combination." Jonkers shrugged. "Thieves are more apt to steal food, booze, lottery tickets, you name it."

The stairs creaked loudly. Dernice and another uniformed officer appeared. After a brief chat to fill him in, the second cop ran back downstairs to monitor the outside of the building.

"You got any lights up here?"

"Unfortunately, no." Dernice told her about Elvira not wanting to spend money to have the wiring fixed.

Jonkers eyed her skeptically. "You can afford high-tech surveillance equipment but you don't have enough money for a minor electrical repair?"

"You have to know my sister to understand," Dernice said.

"It's priorities," Carlita added. "She has her own set of priorities."

"I'm gonna want to look at your recordings after we're done but first." The officer slid the vent latches to the side and slowly removed the cover.

Carlita held her breath, watching as the cop beamed her flashlight inside. "It's clear."

"That's a relief." Dernice swiped her eyebrow. "I was totally freaked out."

"Hang on. Something is in here." She glanced over her shoulder. "Can I borrow your broom?"

Dernice grabbed the broom and handed it to her.

"Thanks." She turned it at an angle and eased it into the opening. "It's stuck."

"What is it?" Pete asked.

"It looks like a piece of fabric." Officer Jonkers set the broom aside. Reaching in as far as she could, she began banging around. "I can't reach it. It's too far down."

Dernice squeezed past her, peering into the opening. "There's something in there, for sure."

The cop scratched her forehead. "Before we get all excited about this being some sort of clue, let's look at your surveillance camera recordings."

Leading the way, Dernice escorted the group to Elvira's office.

Jonkers radioed for her backup to join them. "We're going to take a look at the surveillance."

Dernice made quick work of pulling up the recordings. "Around what time did the burglars break into the pawn shop?"

Carlita and Pete exchanged a quick glance. "It was somewhere around ten or ten thirty."

"Let's see what we have." Humming under her breath, Dernice accessed the front perimeter camera recordings. Sure enough, close to ten forty-five, the same pair appeared. One of them was limping.

"I noticed after they fell from the drainpipe, the climber started limping," Carlita grew quiet, watching as they scoped the place out. The bigger of the two abruptly stopped and looked directly at the camera.

The pair huddled together and then split up, each going in opposite directions and out of camera range. They reappeared and began motioning toward the front of Elvira's building.

Similar to what they had done at the pawn shop, the smaller of the two tossed a rope with a hook on the end up in the air. It fell back down. They threw it a second time. It fell again. Unwilling to give up, they tossed it a third time, and it caught on something.

Tugging on the end, the more athletic of the two began climbing the rope to the second level, but at a slower pace.

"The burglar appears to be favoring their left foot," Officer Jonkers said.

"I was thinking the same." They moved out of recording range into what Carlita believed was the vicinity of the vent cover.

"I can say with almost a hundred percent certainty these are the same two who broke into the store down the street," Jonkers said. "Which means these individuals are more than likely responsible for all three burglaries."

"So." Dernice shifted her feet. "It's safe to assume they were inside the ductwork."

"I think so," Carlita said. "I wonder what time they broke into Colby's place."

"It was after eleven." Jonkers motioned to the other officer. "We need to grab some tools from our toolbox and try to remove the object stuck inside the vent."

After they left, Pete, Carlita and Dernice headed back upstairs to wait.

Dernice stood on her tippy toes and beamed her flashlight inside. "This looks easy."

"What looks easy?"

"Climbing in the vent." She held out her flashlight. "Can you hold this?"

Carlita took it from her. "You can't be serious."

"About crawling in there? Sure I am." Dernice motioned to Pete. "Can you give me a hand?"

"In case you haven't noticed, it's a fairly narrow opening." Pete shifted his stance and laced his fingers together. "Against my better judgment, I'll give you a lift."

"No worries. Believe it or not, I'm a pretty limber gal." Dernice placed both hands on the side of the vent and her foot in Pete's hands, using momentum to lift herself up. "Heave-ho. Here I go."

Chapter 5

Carlita held her breath, watching as Dernice jiggled and wiggled her way into the rectangular air duct.

"It's tight," her voice echoed.

"And a good thing the vent is secured by support braces," Carlita muttered.

Pete adjusted his stance, leveraging his body to give her the extra "umpf" needed to crawl the rest of the way inside. "Have you given any thought to how you're going to get back out?"

"Maybe a big old suction tube," Dernice joked. "Hang on. I can almost reach it."

Her voice grew faint, and Carlita could hear her mumbling under her breath.

POP! A loud popping noise, almost like an air gun going off, blasted through the air.

Carlita's eyes widened as an entire metal panel groaned under her weight. She gritted her teeth, waiting for Dernice to come crashing to the floor.

"I got it!" she hollered. "It's a piece of purple fabric. Help pull me back out."

Pete grasped Dernice's right ankle while Carlita grabbed hold of her left. On the count of three, they both pulled.

Dernice grunted. "Ouch."

"I'm sorry," Carlita apologized. "I thought you were ready for us to pull."

"I'm hung up on a metal band." The wedged woman began panting. "There's not a lot of air in here. I'm feeling a little claustrophobic."

"I bet." Carlita released her grip. "What are we going to do?"

"We should have greased Dernice up before she crawled in," Pete joked.

"Something told me this wasn't going to end well."

"What's going on out there?" she asked. "Are you gonna keep pulling?"

"We'll pull on three. One...two..." At the count of three, Pete and Carlita both tugged, to no avail. The woman was literally stuck.

"Great." Dernice wiggled wildly, causing the ductwork to pop and bang. "I feel like Augustus Gloop."

"Who is Augustus Gloop?" Pete asked.

"From Willie Wonka & the Chocolate Factory," Carlita said. "He was the chunky boy who drank from the chocolate river, fell in and got stuck in the pipe. You've never seen it?"

"Never," Pete said.

"We'll have to watch it sometime. The movie is a lesson about a lot of things—greed, gluttony, overindulgence, all caused by parents who spoiled their children."

"Hellloooo," Dernice hollered. "Can we discuss the merits of Willie's movie some other time? I'm feeling a little lightheaded."

"I might need to get a hacksaw and cut her out."

"Carefully," Dernice said.

"Of course." Pete turned to go, nearly colliding with the officers who were tromping up the steps.

Jonkers held what appeared to be a grabber tool, the kind used for picking up trash on the side of the road. She came to an abrupt halt when she spotted Dernice's sneakers sticking out of the vent. "What's going on?"

"Dernice thought she would save you some trouble and retrieve the potential clue herself," Carlita explained.

"I got it," she confirmed.

Jonkers made a clicking sound with her teeth. "It looks like you got something else."

"I hate to admit it, but I'm afraid I'm stuck."

"We won't need these." The cop waved the grabber tool in the air.

The second officer stepped closer, assessing the situation. "She's wedged in there like a sardine."

"Before we resort to our extraction tool, let's try pulling her out," Jonkers said.

Carlita cleared her throat. "Pete and I have already tried, but you're more than welcome to give it a go."

"Gently," Dernice said.

The officers each grabbed an ankle. Working together, they pulled hard, freeing Dernice to within an inch of her knees. But that was as far as they got.

Jonkers placed her hands on her hips. "She's jammed in there. How did she get wedged in so tightly?"

"It wasn't easy," Dernice joked. "So, now what?"

"I could run home and get my hacksaw," Pete offered.

"It's a thought." Jonkers motioned her partner off to the side and they began talking in low voices.

"What are they saying?" Carlita whispered.

"I have no idea."

"Hey. It's getting quiet out there," Dernice said. "What's going on?"

"We're trying to come up with a plan," Pete said. "Hold tight."

"No worries. I'm not going anywhere."

Thump...thump...thump...thump. A dull thumping sound ensued.

Carlita tiptoed closer. "What is that noise?"

"Me trying to keep calm. I've never been claustrophobic before, but I'm feeling a little uptight."

"On the plus side," Carlita said. "We've confirmed whoever was crawling around in there was fairly thin."

"And agile," Pete added. "Did you see the way they scaled the side of the pawn shop? It was a rookie cat burglar move."

"But why Walton Square? I mean, if I was going to break into businesses, I would target a more upscale side of town," Carlita said.

The conversation ended when the cops finished consulting one another. "Officer Jonkers and I have been given special clearance to use Heidi."

"Who is Heidi?" Pete asked.

"Not who, but what." She looked Pete up and down. "Heidi is hefty. We might need to borrow your muscle to get her up the stairs."

Pete and Carlita exchanged a concerned glance. "We can't leave her there," she finally said.

"True."

She tapped Jonkers on the shoulder. "What exactly is Heidi?" she whispered in her ear.

"A special tool used only in dire circumstances."

Carlita didn't dare ask any other questions. Instead, she attempted to distract Dernice, whose foot was now twitching. "Are you gonna be all right?"

"I hope so. Well, I guess I can knock this little adventure off my bucket list."

Despite the seriousness of the situation, Carlita chuckled. "You had getting stuck in an air vent on your bucket list?"

"No. I was trying to make a joke." Dernice shifted, causing the ductwork to pop again. "My hand is going to sleep."

"Where is your hand?"

"Under my armpit."

"How did? Never mind," Carlita said. "Hopefully, you'll be free soon."

Jonkers, who had been quietly listening, spoke up. "Or stuck in there until we can get the fire department over here."

"What would the fire department do?" Dernice asked.

"You don't want to know. We'll make the call as a last resort."

The men arrived, carrying what looked like a huge pair of pliers. They set them near Dernice's point of entry. The cop reached into his pocket and handed Carlita a pair of earplugs.

"What are these for?"

"Heidi is loud." Officer Jonkers tapped on the metal. "Hey, Dernice, we're going to start working on getting you out of there. Are you able to plug your ears?"

"I can plug my left ear with my finger. My other hand is wedged under my armpit."

Carlita's level of anxiety ramped up a notch when she noticed the officers exchanging a somber glance. Something told her Dernice would deeply regret her impulsive decision to crawl into the narrow vent.

61

Chapter 6

Carlita said the first thing that popped into her head. "Isn't this a little overkill? I mean, can't we just use a regular single blade saw to cut through the metal? It looks pretty flimsy."

"We don't have the right tools." Jonkers told her they could wait for the fire department, who would have what was needed.

"I have a pair of wire snippers in my glovebox." Officer Thryce took off, returning moments later holding a small pair of red snippers.

Carlita wrinkled her nose. "It's gonna take hours to cut through the metal using those."

"I'm feeling kind of lightheaded in here," Dernice said. "Just cut the thing open and get me out."

"We won't be responsible for the damage," Jonkers warned.

"I don't care." Dernice's voice grew faint. "I need fresh air. Can you cut a hole near my face first so I can breathe?"

"Do you need us to call an ambulance?"

"Not yet, but if we keep talking, you might."

"Let's find out exactly where her head is." The cop grabbed the broom and began lightly tapping the bottom of the vent. "Tell me when I'm getting close to your head."

Tap, tap, tap.

"You hit my chin. Keep going."

She tapped a little higher.

"You've reached my forehead."

Pete and Officer Thryce had a brief discussion about where to cut, finally deciding to start a little above her head and carefully work their way down.

Because of the weight of the equipment, it took both men to lift the tool.

"Brace yourself," Thryce said.

"I'm braced."

The cop placed the ends of the giant pliers against the rivets and turned the tool on. It made a loud buzzing sound and shook every inch of the metal structure.

Carlita slid the earplugs in, certain Dernice was going to have a whopper of a headache by the time it was all over.

Working at a slow but steady pace, the men carved out a hole roughly six inches wide. Within seconds, they'd doubled the size. "I think we're close."

Thryce and Pete set Heidi on the floor. Using the red snippers, the cop began cutting his way toward the trapped woman. "I'm almost there. Lift your head if you can."

"Already done." Dernice's voice grew louder. A few more snips and her face, now swollen and red, appeared. "Thank you. You're an angel."

While the cop continued cutting, Pete pulled the section of metal back. As soon as her face was free, they switched ends and began working their way up from her lower legs.

Carlita consulted her watch. Dernice had been trapped inside the vent for well over half an hour.

She began wiggling her feet.

Thryce stopped cutting. "You're gonna have to hold still. I don't want to cut you."

"Sorry." She stopped moving.

Snip. Peel. Snip. Peel. Working together, the men made a straight line along the left-hand side of the ductwork.

Dernice started to slide. Thryce dropped the snippers on the floor and shouldered her weight to keep her from falling. "We need to keep her up until we get both sides cut."

Pete grabbed the tool. Picking up the pace, he worked quickly, cutting away at the other side of the metal. With each snip, Dernice drooped lower and lower.

"We can slide her out now." With Pete on one side and Officer Thryce on the other, they wrapped their arms around her legs and slowly slid her the rest of the way out.

She hit the floor and landed with a dull thud.

Dernice, her face puffy and red, placed her hand on her forehead. "Remind me to never crawl inside an air vent again. Thank you for getting me out." She started to sway.

Carlita put an arm around her. "You look a little red. Are you sure you're okay?"

"I am now. It was a tight fit and I think I was running out of oxygen." Dernice lifted her elbow, revealing a small scratch running along the back of her arm. "I guess this little scrape isn't too bad, considering I was packed in there like a big fluffy sardine."

"I'm glad you didn't come crashing down and land on the floor."

"The good news is I managed to grab this." Dernice unclenched her fist. In it was a purple scrap of fabric. "While I was up there hanging around, I noticed it doesn't have any dust on it."

"Can I see it?"

Dernice handed it to Officer Jonkers.

She examined the silky scrap. "It looks as if this got caught on something and ripped."

"It was wrapped around a rivet. My guess is the burglar, obviously someone smaller than me, crawled through the vent. The material got caught and ripped."

Jonkers folded it in half and dropped it in her pocket. "I'll hang onto this for the investigation."

Pete nudged a chunk of cut metal with the tip of his shoe. "Something tells me Elvira won't be happy about the damage."

"Maybe you can get it repaired before she comes home," Carlita said.

While the others discussed the mangled metal, Officer Thryce unclipped his flashlight and began examining what was left of the ductwork. "The burglars went to a lot of trouble to get inside this place."

"And the pawn shop," Jonkers said. "If this is the work of the same two, their entry point differed slightly from the grocery store burglary. They entered on the ground level."

"I can't be certain, but I believe Ken and his daughter Faith live upstairs," Carlita said.

"They do," Jonkers said. "They also confirmed they were attending the local fundraiser."

"Going back to the theory the burglars knew no one was around."

Jonkers shifted her feet. "From the surveillance videos, we can see where the burglar climbed the side of the building and entered through the vent. I want to take a quick look at the footage again."

"I'll go pull it up." Dernice, Officer Jonkers, and Officer Thryce went downstairs.

Carlita waited until they were gone. She meandered over to the window and peered out. "I see something under a shingle."

Pete craned his neck. "Do you mean the yellow spot on the other side of the vent?"

"Mmm-hmm." Carlita glanced over her shoulder and reached for the window latch.

"What are you doing?"

"I want to find out what it is."

"I'll go." Pete opened the window. Balancing on the sill, he swung his right leg over the side and climbed out.

"Be careful." Carlita clasped her hands, warily eyeing the overhang that sloped at a sharp angle.

"I will." Taking small steps, he inched closer to the yellow object. "Almost there."

Pete reached down to grab it. His right foot slipped. He started sliding.

Carlita lunged forward, desperately trying to grab hold of him.

"Whoa." With arms flailing, Pete managed to regain his balance. "The roof pitch is steeper than it looks." Moving cautiously and keeping his right hand on the wall for balance, he leaned down and picked up the small object.

"What is it?"

"A ticket."

Carlita's breath caught in her throat when she got a closer look, easily recognizing the slip of paper in his hand. "Will you look at that?"

Chapter 7

"It's a raffle ticket." Carlita took the ticket from her husband. "A hundred bucks says this is from our fundraiser."

"Hey." Dernice and the cops appeared at the top of the stairs. "We thought we lost you."

"We noticed this wedged under a shingle." Carlita held it up.

"I'm by no means an expert on criminals, although admittedly I've been around more than my share," Dernice said. "I have to say, this has to be one of the most bungled burglaries I've ever seen. The perps are leaving clues all over the place."

"It's beginning to look that way," Carlita said. "They break into the pawn shop through a window to nowhere. They come over here, get caught on the vent duct and then leave a ticket on the roof."

"Does Elvira have a safe downstairs?" Pete asked.

"Yeah." Dernice told them she and the cops had already checked it out. "It probably wouldn't hurt to take another look around. For all we know, these clowns may have left more clues behind."

Officer Jonkers removed a tissue from her pocket and held it out. "I'll need to hang onto the raffle ticket. It could be potential evidence."

Carlita hesitated. "Before you confiscate it, I want to snap a photo to see if I can confirm this is from Steve's fundraiser." Using her cell phone, she took a picture of the front and back.

Officer Thryce, who had left to take a look around, reappeared. "From what I can tell, it doesn't look like the burglars bothered with the other rooms up here. What else is in this building besides offices?"

"Our home. My sister and I live here."

The group returned to the first floor. "I'll show you our apartment." Dernice and the officers strolled out of the office area and into the back.

Pete glanced at the open laptop sitting on Elvira's desk. "While we wait, let's take another look at the surveillance recording."

Carlita peered over his shoulder, watching the burglars check out the front of Elvira's building. "Maybe I'm reading too much into it, but don't you think it's odd how instead of busting out a window on the ground level, the burglars kept going up to the second floor?"

"It does seem unusual," Pete agreed. "They appear to be in good physical condition, at least the one who scaled the wall is."

"Almost athletic," Carlita murmured. "Clearly, they noticed the cameras. One of them looked directly at it."

"Noticed, but didn't care."

"Because they knew no one was around."

Muffled voices grew louder. Dernice and the cops reappeared. "The place is clean. Whoever got in either didn't want to bother spending the time

73

tearing the place apart or got spooked and left in a hurry."

"Or couldn't find anything worth stealing." Jonkers glanced at her watch. "My partner and I need to finish writing our reports. We'll be back to wrap things up."

Dernice escorted them out. She caught up with Pete and Carlita, who were still standing near Elvira's desk. "I gotta admit, this has me scratching my head. I mean, they didn't steal any electronics or computers. They didn't touch the petty cash drawer."

"They didn't get anything from the pawn shop either," Carlita said. "Although if they had actually broken into the store, they would have found some goods worth stealing."

The officers reappeared. They gave Dernice a copy of their preliminary report and asked her to let them know if she found anything else missing, disturbed, or if other potential clues surfaced before leaving.

Carlita stifled a yawn. "It's way past my bedtime. I say we call it a day."

Dernice trailed behind and followed them out onto the sidewalk. "I texted Luigi while we were waiting. He's gonna come over and hang out tonight in case the burglars decide to come back."

"It's always best to be cautious, especially knowing they're still out there somewhere," Carlita said. "I'm going to drop by Ken's store tomorrow. I'll let you know if I find anything out."

"What about the ticket?" Dernice asked.

She patted her pocket. "I have a photo. I'll run by Shades of Ink while I'm at it to see if there's a match."

"I'm sure Jonkers or Thryce will do the same," Pete said. "I would suggest leaving the investigation to the police, but I might as well save my breath."

"It bothers me to think someone from the fundraiser had the nerve to bust into Walton

Square businesses while we were helping Steve and Paisley."

"It's definitely a scummy move." Dernice let them out the front door and locked it behind them.

During their walk home, Carlita mulled over the clues. By all accounts, the burglars were not professionals. Not by a longshot. She could understand why the pawn shop was targeted, possibly even the grocery store, but why Elvira's place?

"Do you think…" Her voice trailed off.

"Think what?" Pete prompted.

"Nothing. I'm thinking out loud. It's so far out there, I don't even know if it makes sense."

"About the burglaries?"

"Yeah. I'm trying to figure out why they targeted Elvira's place."

"Because it was only a stone's throw away from the pawn shop and they thought—what the heck…we're already here, we might as well try breaking in there too," Pete said. "What's your theory?"

"You know how obsessed Elvira is with finding treasure. Maybe she's been bragging about it to the wrong people. They broke in to see if they could find anything," Carlita said.

"It's a thought. Definitely a possibility," Pete said. "We know why the pawn shop was hit."

"And maybe even Colby's if they were looking for quick cash, booze, cigarettes, or lottery tickets, like Officer Jonkers pointed out."

The couple reached the Parrot House Restaurant, which had long since closed for the day.

"I'm going to take a quick look around outside, just to be sure we weren't targeted too."

"I'll wait here," Carlita said.

"Actually." Pete unlocked the door. "I would feel better if you waited inside."

77

Touched by her husband's concern, Carlita bounced on the tips of her toes and kissed his cheek. "Have I told you lately how much I love you, Pete Taylor?"

"I believe so. But I never get tired of hearing it." He gave her a playful pat on the back. "I'm sure Rambo is itching to stretch his legs. I'll give a holler as soon as I'm finished. We'll walk him together."

"Be careful." Carlita reached the top of the stairs and found her pup waiting near the door. "I know you're raring to go out, but we gotta wait for Pete."

Heavy footsteps echoed. Her husband appeared. "I'm ready."

"Well?" Carlita and Rambo followed him down the steps and into the yard.

"All is well on the home and restaurant front," Pete reported. "Hopefully, the burglars didn't target anyone else at the fundraiser."

"I'll check around in the morning." Carlita's eyelids drooped. "I'm whupped."

"Me too. Let's call it a day."

Back inside, the couple took turns getting ready for bed. Pete finished first. Carlita wasn't far behind. She tiptoed into the bedroom and found him stretched out in their bed, his eyes closed and sound asleep.

As quietly as possible, she turned his bedside lamp off, crept over to her side, and slid under the covers.

Despite being exhausted, her thoughts were racing, hopscotching from the fundraiser to the break-in at the pawn shop to Dernice getting stuck in the air vent.

She thought about Elvira and wondered if the burglars broke into her place looking for treasure. One thing was certain, whoever they were, they knew, or at least suspected, no one was around, leaving the businesses wide open and easy marks. Except for the surveillance cameras. Elvira had more surveillance equipment than Fort Knox. Savannah Swag had almost as much, yet it hadn't deterred the burglars.

There was something about the break-ins that wasn't sitting right with Carlita, although she couldn't put her finger on what it was.

Perhaps tomorrow, after a good night's sleep and a little investigation, she could glean additional clues. First on the list was figuring out if the raffle ticket was from the fundraiser. If so, they might be able to nail the burglars before they struck again.

Chapter 8

Early the next morning, Pete gathered some supplies to secure the broken window before he and Carlita drove over to the pawn shop.

While he started working on the repair, Carlita ran inside to track her son down.

She found a bleary-eyed Tony seated at his desk, the norm now that baby Melody, the newest member of the Garlucci family, had arrived...and what a beautiful baby she was.

"I would ask how you slept last night, but I'm guessing not much," Carlita teased.

"You guessed right. Although I will say we're thankful Melody is on a regular feeding schedule." Tony rubbed his eyes. "I think she has some sixth sense because it seems like as soon as I fall asleep after her feedings, she wakes right back up."

"It's a vicious cycle." She patted his arm. "The good news is before you know it, your little angel will sleep for longer and longer stretches. Remember, she's trying to adjust to her new environment."

"I'm not complaining. The stinker has me wrapped around her little finger." Tony leaned his elbows on the counter. "I was gonna give you a call but figured you would stop by with news about last night's fundraiser. How much did we raise?"

"Over seventeen thousand dollars."

Tony whistled loudly. "Seventeen grand. Good for them."

"Steve was so excited. I couldn't be prouder of our close-knit Savannah community," Carlita said. "Unfortunately, not everyone was there to help."

"What do you mean?"

"I'll show you." She led Tony through the pawn shop, out the front door and to the side where Pete stood on the ladder, cleaning out the rest of the broken glass from the windowsill.

"What the…"

"We noticed it last night on our way home."

"Someone broke the window to nowhere," Tony said.

"They also busted the drainpipe on the way down, which will need to be fixed. We caught them on camera." Carlita gave him the general timeframe. "Officer Jonkers came by. I'm not sure if you remember her."

"From the Christmas boat parade a few years ago when Brittney's bodyguard got snuffed out?"

"Yeah. You have a good memory," she said. "Anyway, after she took the report, Pete and I walked around the block to make sure nothing else had been hit."

"And?"

"Elvira's place was also broken into."

"By the same people?"

"We believe so. One of the burglars scaled the wall and climbed in through an upper level air vent," Carlita said. "Colby's Corner Store also got hit."

"No kidding. All three were burglarized last night?"

"During the fundraiser." Carlita turned her cell phone on and pulled up the photo she'd taken of the raffle ticket they found wedged under the shingle. "We found this on Elvira's overhang."

"It looks like one of our raffle tickets. So, whoever broke in figured they wouldn't get caught."

"That's what we're thinking." Carlita told him she planned to check with the other Walton Square business owners to see if anyone else had been burglarized.

"They're not very good thieves. First of all, we got cameras everywhere."

"Cameras which recorded them, not to mention they left clues behind—the raffle ticket and a scrap of fabric that got caught inside the ductwork."

"Too bad they didn't get stuck," Tony joked.

"No, but Dernice did."

"Did what?"

"Got stuck inside the vent, trying to get the piece of fabric."

His jaw dropped. "Dernice crawled into the air duct?"

"And had to be rescued. It was a mess."

Pete made his way down the ladder. "I'm ready to put the plywood up. I hate to say it, but this might cost you a few coins. These old windows aren't standard size. Ask me how I know."

"Because you've had to replace some of yours," Carlita said.

"Yep." Pete dusted his hands. "I'll need some help in getting the plywood secured."

"You got it."

Tracking down another ladder and working together, Tony and Pete carried the piece to the top. While Tony held the plywood, Pete nailed it in place.

They returned to the sidewalk and stood back to inspect their handiwork.

"Thanks for covering the window," Tony said. "I'll start making some calls to get a window company out here to give us a quote."

"If you need help let me know." Carlita told him she and Pete had done a preliminary check of their properties the previous night. "I don't think we overlooked anything, but it might not be a bad idea to triple check to make sure the place is locked up tight tonight."

"You know it." Tony helped Pete carry his stuff back to the truck while Carlita trailed behind.

"I need to check in at Ravello's," she said. "I figured I would stop by Mercedes' place to find out if she noticed anything. I'll also swing by Steve's tattoo shop to see if I can confirm we have a match on the ticket we found."

"I figured as much." Pete sneaked in a kiss. "I've made plans for us this evening, so don't gallivant around too late."

"What plans?"

He pressed his finger to her lips. "It's a surprise."

"You know how I feel about surprises."

"You'll like this one," he promised.

"Fine. I like being pleasantly surprised," Carlita said. "I'm hoping we get lucky and these rookie burglars left more clues behind."

After Pete left and Tony headed back inside the pawn shop, Carlita trekked to the restaurant to check in. She found Arnie, her head manager, prepping for lunch.

Carlita thanked him for all his hard work handling the food for the fundraiser. They chatted for a few minutes before she took off. Her next stop was her daughter's place.

Reaching the second-floor apartment, she knocked on the door. When Mercedes didn't answer, Carlita, thinking she wasn't home, turned to go.

The door flew open. Mercedes appeared, her hair standing on end and looking as if she had just crawled out of bed. "Hey, Ma."

"Hey, Mercedes. I'm sorry if I woke you."

"It's okay. I needed to get my butt out of bed. What's up?"

Carlita briefly filled her daughter in. "I'm almost positive the ticket we found was from last night. I'm gonna swing by Steve's place to see if it's a match."

"I kept track of the tickets and have all the numbers." Mercedes ushered her mother inside. "I put them in a spreadsheet."

Carlita's heart skipped a beat. "Awesome. Can you tell me who got what tickets?"

"Unfortunately, no. There's no way to tell who bought which ticket."

"Bummer."

Mercedes plopped down in front of her computer. She turned it on and logged in, pulling up a spreadsheet full of numbered columns. "It might take a minute. I don't have every single number, only the run numbers."

"The run numbers?" Carlita echoed.

"You know...starting at number one and ending at a hundred. I'll show you what I mean." Mercedes tapped the keys and zoomed in on the spreadsheet. "I kept track of who got what number run. For instance, the pawn shop had a certain set of tickets. Pete's restaurant and his pirate ship had another. Ravello's was a different series."

"Ah." Carlita arched her eyebrow. "I had no idea you kept track of where each roll of tickets went."

"The goal was to keep the winners honest. You never know when someone might try to slip a few fakes in and win a prize without buying a raffle ticket."

Carlita playfully nudged her. "I think you've been writing too many crime novels."

"Hey, I'm sure it happens." Mercedes grabbed a pen and notepad. "What's the number?"

Carlita tracked down the photo she'd taken and rattled it off.

"Got it."

Mercedes enlarged the screen and began making her way down the list. Row after row of tickets had gone out, not only to the businesses in Walton Square, but all over town.

"Wow. I had no idea you handed out all these tickets."

"Paisley and I went door to door," Mercedes chuckled. "We even went back to a few businesses who didn't say yes right away. I think they got tired of seeing us."

"All of our hard work paid off to the tune of over seventeen thousand dollars."

"Isn't it sweet?" Mercedes beamed. "Steve and Paisley texted me last night, thanking me again for helping."

"I got the same text. I would hope if we were ever in the same position, our friends and neighbors would help us out, too." Carlita squinted her eyes. "No match yet?"

"I'm getting near the end. Looking back, it would have made more sense for me to put them in numerical order versus alphabetical order by business name."

"I think you did great. The fact you have this list is nothing short of a miracle," Carlita said.

Mercedes grew quiet, scrolling through the list. "We're down to The Flying Gunner, so we're getting close to the end."

"Hang on." Carlita tapped the screen. "I think you passed the series this ticket might have been in."

Mercedes scrolled back up. "Here it is. You were right, Ma. This ticket was from the fundraiser."

"That's not all." Carlita's scalp tingled when she noticed who had been given the roll of tickets. "I think we may have found our first clue."

Chapter 9

"This ticket was sold at the fundraiser, not by a Walton Square business," Carlita said.

"Which means whoever lost the ticket on top of Elvira's roof was there last night." Mercedes absentmindedly tugged on a stray strand of hair.

"The bad news is we had tons of people there."

"The place was jam-packed." Mercedes began scribbling on her notepad. "Paisley and I were in charge of selling the tickets. I can confirm we sold a lot."

"Figuring out who had this ticket will be like searching for a needle in a haystack," Carlita sighed.

"We can drill down a little and find out what the raffle item was." She flipped to another tab and pulled up the long list of goodies. "The ticket was purchased for a chance to win Colby's Corner Store's $200 gift basket."

"Was the ticket a winner?"

"Nope."

"Interesting." Carlita paced. "Colby's was also broken into. I wonder if there's a connection."

"Maybe the burglars were ticked that they didn't win the raffle and decided to break into the store to get some free goods."

"What about the pawn shop and Elvira's place?"

"I can understand the pawn shop, but why Elvira's?" Mercedes wrinkled her nose. "Maybe they got mixed up and thought they were burglarizing a place which actually had something worth stealing."

"Could be. Based on how sloppy they were, I think it would be safe to say they weren't professional thieves."

"I wonder…"

"Wonder what?" Carlita prompted.

"I don't want to come across as being judgmental."

"You're wondering if maybe one of Steve's clients or friends might have been behind it." Carlita sucked in a breath. "I hate to admit it, but the thought had crossed my mind last night. A few of them were a little rough around the edges."

"Some of the nicest, most honest people are covered in tattoos."

"While some of the nastiest, most judgmental people are viewed as upstanding citizens of society," Carlita said. "I know, and I agree. The fact of the matter is the only thing we know for certain is one of the criminals was in pretty good physical shape. They were sloppy, and they were there last night."

"I guess the next step would be to talk to Steve and Ken Colby."

"Which is where I'm heading now." Carlita thanked her daughter. "I won't take up anymore of your time."

"You're not bothering me. Actually, I wouldn't mind tagging along."

"The more the merrier."

Mercedes threw on sweatpants and a T-shirt. She grabbed her keys before following her mother down the stairs and to the end of the alley.

Making a sharp left, the women strolled along the sidewalk to Steve's tattoo shop, only to discover the lights were off and the doors were locked.

"Crud. They're not around."

"Steve and Paisley are probably still recuperating from last night's shindig," Mercedes joked.

Carlita glanced at her watch. "It's early. Let's head to Colby's. I know the grocery store is open."

Continuing on, they rounded the corner, reaching the entrance to the neighborhood's popular specialty store. The overhead bell chimed, announcing their arrival.

A quick check of the cozy, charming interior, most of which you could see from the entrance, found Faith, Ken's daughter, standing near the cash register. Her father stood behind the bakery counter near the back.

"I see Ken." It was a straight shot down the center aisle. Carlita caught his eye and gave a friendly wave.

"Good morning, Carlita."

"Good morning. We didn't get much of a chance to talk at Steve's fundraiser last night. It was so hectic. I wanted to thank you for your donation and for supporting our small community."

"You're welcome. It's a shame the evening had to end on such a sour note."

Faith finished ringing up a customer's purchases and hurried over. "Are you telling Carlita and Mercedes about what happened?"

"How the store was burglarized?" Mercedes asked. "It's the other reason why Ma and I are here. Officer Jonkers told us this place was broken into."

"Along with your pawn shop. What did they take?"

"Nothing. Although they managed to bust out an upstairs window." Carlita told them it was a window to nowhere. "I guess they weren't dumb enough to keep going and break into the pawn shop."

Ken told them he and Faith were on their way home last night when they heard the security alarm going off at the end of the block. "I knew right away it was this place."

"The alarm didn't scare them off?"

"No." Faith shook her head. "We did."

"Did what?" Carlita asked.

"Scared them off."

Mercedes made a choking sound. "You saw whoever broke in?"

"Saw them. Chased after them," Ken said. "They probably would have moved faster if not for the fact they were trying not to drop the loot they stole and one of them was limping."

Carlita's jaw dropped. "Limping? I knew it. This proves it's the same two. The climber fell from my drainpipe. What did they take?"

"I have a copy of the police report." Faith excused herself. She returned a short time later and handed Carlita a piece of paper.

"Thanks." She slipped her reading glasses on and studied the sheet. "Vitamins, supplements and energy drinks. This seems like an unusual combination. Was there anything else?"

"A bag of pork rinds."

"Pork rinds?" Mercedes blinked rapidly. "I guess they got hungry."

"All their burglarizing must have worked up an appetite." Carlita handed the report back to Faith.

"I thought they were kind of odd choices myself," Ken said. "The chip of choice is typically Doritos or potato chips. They didn't touch the popular stuff…booze, cigarettes or lottery tickets."

"It was an unusual burglary," Faith said.

"How so?"

"They didn't even try to steal the safe."

"Because it's bolted to the floor," Ken said. "They would need some heavy duty tools to cut through it."

"Or maybe they didn't get that far," Carlita said. "If you scared them off, you may have prevented them from stealing more or doing even worse damage. What did they look like?"

"Both were wearing dark clothing. As I mentioned, one of them had a limp. They hightailed it out of here as soon as they saw us," Ken said. "The thinner of the two set the pace."

"Which was at a pretty quick clip," Faith said. "I guess they were surprised when we showed up."

Carlita's eyes narrowed. "Hang on. What time did you leave Steve's place?"

"It was close to half past eleven," Ken said. "I remember telling Faith I wanted to catch the late-night weather forecast because I planned to go fishing today."

"But had to cancel because of the burglary." Carlita frowned. "I'm sorry your good deed backfired."

"It's not your fault. So, when did the break-in occur?"

Carlita gave him the timeline of when the pawn shop window was busted and Elvira's place was broken into. "They went from my place to Elvira's and then maybe over here."

"I know this might sound like a dumb question, but why Elvira's place?" Faith asked. "I get why they would want to get into this place and the pawn

101

shop, but what would a security services company have that they could want?"

"Gems, gold, booty," Mercedes said. "It wouldn't surprise me if Elvira told anyone and everyone who will listen that she's searching for gold."

"Ah." Faith clasped her hands. "You're right. She's pretty well-known around here for her treasure hunting."

"And for breaking into tunnels, digging up her yard, chipping away at her basement walls," Carlita said. "She could have inadvertently put a target on her back."

"Would you like to see our camera's surveillance recordings?"

"If it's not too much trouble."

"Not at all." Ken ushered them back to the storage room, where he accessed the footage. He tracked down the timeframe in question and hit the play button.

Although the images were grainy and dark, Carlita was almost certain the burglars were the same ones. "Where did they break in?"

Ken took them outside to the sidewalk. He spun around and pointed to the alley. "There's a small bathroom window back there. They broke the glass and climbed in."

"Can we take a closer look?"

"Sure."

Walking single file, they approached the window, now covered with a sheet of plywood. "They tossed a rock through the window, flipped the lock and let themselves in."

Carlita studied the opening. "The thinner of the two could have easily climbed in here."

"With a little heave-ho help from their partner in crime," Mercedes said. "Would this have triggered the alarm?"

"Nope." He explained as soon as they stepped into the hall, it activated the motion sensor. "The burglars made it about ten steps before the alarm went off."

"I wonder if anyone else in Walton Square was broken into." Carlita made a mental note to email their neighbors and thanked Ken for showing her the footage. "There is a final clue. We found a raffle ticket on Elvira's roof."

"From the fundraiser?"

"Yeah. I kept a list of tickets, what rolls were given to who." Mercedes told him the ticket was sold during the event. "The ticket Ma found was for your gift basket."

Ken stared at her in disbelief. "Are you sure?"

"Positive."

"Interesting." His expression grew grim. "This is all starting to make sense."

Chapter 10

"How is the burglary starting to make sense?" Mercedes asked.

"Whoever broke into our businesses knew we were at Steve's place."

"We were thinking the same thing. Now that we confirmed the ticket we found is from the fundraiser and sold during the event, my guess is the burglars or at least one of them showed up to scope the place out, figure out who was there and maybe even bought a ticket to make it look good."

Carlita picked up. "After purchasing the ticket, they started making their rounds. The pawn shop, Elvira's place, your store."

"But they didn't plan on me and Faith leaving a few minutes early to come home," Ken said. "I agree.

We need to ask around to find out if anyone else was hit."

Carlita thanked him for the information and he promised to let her know if they stumbled upon any other potential clues. She caught up with Mercedes, who had stopped by the front counter to tell Faith goodbye.

"I hope they catch these burglars," his daughter said. "I don't like the idea of them lurking around our neighborhood."

"Me either," Carlita said. "Although if they have half a brain, I doubt they'll be back here, trying to break in."

Exiting the store, mother and daughter backtracked. They reached Shades of Ink tattoo shop and noticed the lights were on. Through the window, Carlita could see Steve standing at the counter.

He caught her eye and hurried to the door to let them in. "Hey, Carlita, Mercedes."

"Hey, Steve. How's it going?"

"It was going great until the cops showed up a little while ago to ask me about some break-ins in our neighborhood last night."

"The pawn shop, Elvira's place and Colby's Corner Store." Carlita filled him in on what they knew. "The bottom line is we think whoever broke in was here last night."

"Scumbags." His eyes flashed with anger. "I hope they catch them."

"Us too. I'm sure the investigators checked out your camera recordings while they were here."

"They did. There's a lot of footage. We didn't have time to go over every second of it, so I forwarded copies to them."

"Which may or may not help," Mercedes said. "There were a lot of people here."

"A ton." Steve shifted his feet. "You mentioned you found a ticket and linked it back to the rolls we had here."

"We did. The purchaser bought a ticket for Colby's $200 gift basket."

"So maybe Ken was the target," Steve guessed. "They didn't win, got ticked and decided to help themselves to his merchandise."

"Or it could be a coincidence." Carlita told him they planned to email the Walton Square business neighbors to find out if anyone else had been burglarized.

"We can do it while you're here," he said. "In fact, I was getting ready to email thank-you notes and have the list up on my computer." He tapped the keys. "What do you want to say?"

"I don't want to alarm them," Carlita said.

"But we also want them to be on guard," Mercedes chimed in.

"True. I'll thank them and mention the burglaries."
Steve grew quiet, focusing his attention on the
screen.

Tappity...tap...tap...tap. "And...send."

"You can type almost as fast as me," Mercedes
teased.

Steve flexed his fingers. "I use the keyboard to
exercise my fingers. It helps keep them limber and
steady when I'm tattooing."

"Interesting. I never knew there was tattoo finger
training," Carlita joked.

"Paisley taught me that little trick."

Carlita looked around. "Where is Paisley?"

"She's covering a shift over at Ravello's."

"I've been so busy with the fundraiser I haven't kept
track of the restaurant."

Steve sobered. "Thanks again, Carlita. You have no
idea how much pressure this took off Paisley and
me."

"You're welcome."

His computer *pinged*. "I'm already getting replies to the email."

Carlita slipped in behind him. "Mind if I look over your shoulder?"

"Not at all." Working his way from the top, Steve clicked on each of the replies. All sent heartfelt messages with words of encouragement. Several expressed concern over the burglaries, but none mentioned being broken into.

He finished going through them. "It looks like you, Ken and Elvira, were the lucky ones. I meant to ask. What did they steal?"

"Nothing from the pawn shop. As far as Dernice can tell, nothing is missing from Elvira's place. Ken said they stole a bag of pork rinds, some vitamins, supplements and energy drinks."

"No cash or booze?"

"Nope."

Carlita's cell phone chimed. It was a text from Shelby, asking if she still planned to stop by to see the baby. She quickly texted back, promising she and Mercedes were on the way. "We need to get going."

Steve followed them to the door. "Would you like me to forward my camera recordings of the party to you?"

"If it's not too much work."

"Not at all. I'll be happy to."

Carlita thanked him, and she and Mercedes took off. During the short walk back to the apartment, the women threw out ideas about why the three businesses were hit.

"Let's try to figure this out." Mercedes lifted a finger. "Ravello's wouldn't be a good target. Neither would Sandy Sue's Bar-B-Que. There's not much in a real estate office that would be worth breaking in for. Ditto for an ice cream shop or Pete's pirate ship."

"True. I suppose our place and Colby's would be higher up on the list."

"Maybe it was all about location," Mercedes said. "All three are in close proximity to each other."

Carlita pondered her daughter's theories. "And after they got caught breaking into Colby's, the burglars got spooked."

Mercedes tapped the side of her forehead. "You gotta think like the thugs and try to put yourself in their shoes."

"They certainly don't seem to be professionals. Hopefully, it was a random act and won't happen again."

Shelby must have been waiting for them because as soon as they reached her apartment, the door flew open. She stood holding baby Melody. Big sister Violet was by her side.

"Nana." The young girl threw her arms around her grandmother.

Carlita knelt next to her and gave her a big hug. "How's my Violet today?"

"I'm good. Melody is kinda cranky."

Mercedes covered her mouth to hide her smile. "Uh-oh. Why is she cranky?"

Violet lifted both hands and shrugged. "I think she has gas."

"She's been doing a lot of burping," Shelby said.

The baby whimpered, and she began rocking her back and forth.

Carlita took Melody from her mother, noticing the dark circles under her daughter-in-law's eyes. "I have today off. Why don't you let me spend a few hours with Melody and Violet over at my place so you can have a break?"

"I..." Shelby hesitated. "Violet wasn't exaggerating. The baby is cranky. Are you sure?"

"I'm positive." Carlita cradled the infant. "I might be a little rusty at baby care, but I'm sure it'll come back quickly."

"To be honest, a nap sounds wonderful. I'm exhausted."

"I'll help Ma," Mercedes offered. "I might have to cover a shift at the restaurant but it won't be until later."

Carlita smoothed Violet's hair. "Why don't you help Mommy gather up some stuff for Melody and art supplies for you?"

"Okay." Violet ran off to pack her things.

Shelby gave Carlita a grateful hug. "I hope you know what you're getting yourself into."

The baby, who had stopped crying, began fussing again.

Carlita grinned. "We'll be fine. Melody, Mercedes, Violet and I are going to have a grand old time."

"I'll go check on Violet." Shelby hurried off. She returned moments later, carrying an overstuffed baby bag. Violet, with her favorite pink and purple backpack on her back, sneaked past her mother, dragging a large tote bag behind her. "I have games, art supplies and even some snacks."

Her mother made a timeout. "Hold on. You only need one bag."

"But I have a lot of stuff. I want to show Nana and Aunt Mercedes my new sketch pad and scented markers."

"It's all right," Carlita chuckled. "Mercedes has an extra hand."

"Melody just ate, so you should be good for a couple of hours." Shelby gave her the next feeding time.

"Got it." Mercedes reached for the baby's bag and Violet's extra tote chock-full of goodies. "Instead of going all the way over to Ma's, we can hang out at my place."

"And play," Violet added.

"Yes. Lots of play. I used to have a box of scented markers." Mercedes leaned down and whispered in her ear. "The cherry is my favorite."

Violet beamed. "Mine too. We can share."

"If you're going to take all of this, why don't you borrow our wagon." Shelby grabbed the handle of a red wagon and steered it into the alley. "This thing is great for hauling the kid's gear around town."

"Thank you. I think it will work perfectly."

"You'll need Melody's baby bouncer and a bottle. Like I said, she'll start fussing in a couple of hours." She ran inside and returned carrying a bouncer and a travel bag. After Violet and Mercedes loaded the rest of the gear, Shelby flipped the bouncer upside down and placed it on top. "Are you positive you want to do this?"

"Absolutely." Carlita shifted her tiny granddaughter to her other arm. "We'll be fine. Rest, relax, recharge. Take a nap or a long hot bubble bath, or maybe even both."

"I will. Nap first and then maybe a bath. It will be like heaven." Shelby thanked them again. "Call if you need anything."

"We will." Carlita tightened her grip on the baby and waited for her daughter to steer the wagon into the alley. "Are you ready for this?"

"I hope so." Mercedes laughed out loud. "If not, something tells me I'm in for a crash course in childcare."

Chapter 11

"First things first. Let's set the baby bouncer on the floor and get little Melody nice and comfy." Balancing the baby in her right arm, Carlita plucked the bouncer from the wagon and placed it near the sofa.

"I can help." Violet dragged her oversized bag of art supplies across the room and dumped them out in the middle of the living room floor.

"You have a lot of neat stuff," Mercedes said.

"I'm gonna share everything with you. But first I have to get it all organized." The young girl began singing a little ditty about flowers and rainbows while placing sketch pads on the coffee table. Up next was her box of scented markers she carefully set between the sketch pads. "Nana can take care of Melody while you and I draw pictures."

"Are you hungry? Would you like a snack?"

"I brought some fruit yummies." Violet cast her aunt a sly side glance and Carlita could almost see the wheels spinning. "What do you have?"

"I'm not sure. Let me look." Mercedes darted into the kitchen and began rummaging around in the cupboards.

Violet, momentarily forgetting about unpacking her supplies, trailed after her.

"I have a can of sardines."

The young girl's eyes widened in horror. "Yuck."

Carlita chuckled. Mercedes caught her mother's eye and winked. "What about creamed spinach? I can warm it up on the stove or if you're really hungry, I'll pop it in the microwave."

"Ew." Violet clutched her small tummy. "No wonder you're so skinny. You should buy better food."

Her grandmother couldn't resist. "What do you think is better food?"

"Skittles. Popsicles, stuff like that."

Melody balled up her fist and began sucking on it. She let out a loud belch, right in Carlita's face.

"Whew." She turned away. "Your mom was right. Melody has the burpies."

"The stinky burpies." Violet patted the top of the counter. "It's okay Aunt Mercedes. I'm not hungry."

"I was kidding. I'm sure I have some snacks you'll like." Mercedes took her hand and led her into the kitchen to a basket of fresh fruit sitting on the counter. "How does a banana or an apple sound?"

"An apple." Violet began singing another song, this one about penguins and porcupines, while her aunt sliced the fruit.

"Here you go." Mercedes placed the wedges in a bowl and handed it to her.

"Thank you."

"You're welcome."

The two returned to the coffee table. Before they got down to the business of creating their masterpieces, Violet insisted her aunt sniff every single marker.

Meanwhile, Carlita and her new granddaughter moseyed around the living room. The baby settled down a bit, but every so often she burped. A sour milk smell accompanied the burps.

She didn't seem fussy and stared wide-eyed at everything Carlita showed her. Melody's small head bobbed as she turned her attention to her grandmother, intently studying her face.

Carlita ran a light finger across her soft, chubby cheek. "You're such a little sweetie pie," she cooed. "Like your big sister, Violet."

She placed the infant in her bouncy seat, tracked down her cell phone, and snapped a picture. Carlita took several photos of Mercedes and Violet before checking her email.

Several of the other area business owners had sent group replies to Steve's email, all confirming they hadn't been visited by burglars. They thanked him and promised to be extra vigilant in case the thieves came back for round two.

She finished scrolling before tapping out a quick text to Pete, letting him know she was at Mercedes' place babysitting. Her stomach grumbled, reminding her she hadn't eaten all day. "I don't know about you, but I'm getting kinda hungry."

"Me too."

"Me three." Violet held her sketch pad up. "I finished my picture for you, Nana."

Carlita took the drawing from her and admired the stick figures. One was a small stick figure with purple hair. The figure stood next to a larger stick figure with clunky oval shoes, short black hair and bright red lips. "Let me guess…this is you and me."

"Yep." Violet beamed. "Do you see Rambo?"

Sure enough, Rambo...or at least the stick version of her pup, stood by her side, his eyes huge black orbs and his tail twice the size of his body.

"I love it. I can't wait to take it home and hang it on the fridge." Carlita kissed the top of her head. "Why don't I order food from the restaurant? We can head over to Morrell Park for a picnic lunch."

"What about Rambo?" Violet asked.

"We can even swing by the house and get Rambo." Carlita eyed the baby, who was still watching her intently. "Unfortunately, we'll need a stroller for Melody. I don't want to disturb your mom in case she's taking a nap."

"Daddy has a buggy at work. We take Melody for walks when she gets fussy."

"You're right. I remember seeing it the other day." Carlita placed a to-go order for them and then she and Mercedes began packing a separate bag of items they thought they might need for their impromptu outing.

The baby clenched her fists and kicked her feet. Mercedes promptly picked her up. She stopped fussing; her gaze laser-focused on her aunt while she talked. "There's my little merry Melody," Mercedes sang. "You and Violet are such cutie pies."

Belch. Melody burped loudly, blowing it right in Mercedes' face.

She gasped. "What on earth was that?"

Violet, noticing the look of shock on her aunt's face, started giggling. "You got one of Melody's icky burpies."

"No kidding." Mercedes frantically waved her hand in front of her face, noticing the baby was trying to smile. "I think she thinks it's funny."

"Her tummy is probably feeling better, getting all the bad gasses out," Carlita cooed, lightly rubbing the top of her head. "At least it's not coming out the other end."

"Not yet," Mercedes grimaced.

124

"She has some bad rooty toots," Violet said.

"Rooty toots?"

"Stinky toots. Daddy calls them blowouts." The young girl plugged her nose. "They're ickier than the burpies."

"Such a small thing to have such a powerful smell." Mercedes started to hand the baby to her mother, which must've triggered another burping episode. She let loose a delicate burp. Although small in sound, it was big on smell.

Poor Mercedes was at the right angle and breathed in the odor. She made a gagging sound and started to heave.

Carlita quickly took the baby from her daughter.

Mercedes doubled over, clutching her gut and dry heaving. "That...was the worst smell I've ever breathed."

"I never realized you had such sensitive gag reflexes," her mother said. "If you think her burps are bad, the rooty toots I'm sure are much worse."

"Lots worse," Violet confirmed.

"I need air." Mercedes flung the front door open and stepped into the hall.

Violet ran after her.

Carlita and the baby trailed behind. "You'll need to go back for the baby bag."

"Do we have to have it?"

Her mother rolled her eyes. "Good heavens. Hold your breath."

"Good idea." Mercedes ran inside and returned in a flash, travel bag in hand. "I can still smell it. I think the smell is trapped in my nostrils."

"You're so dramatic sometimes." Reaching the main floor landing, they stopped by the pawn shop. Carlita found the stroller in the back, tucked in between the desk and the coat rack.

Tony stood off to the side talking to an employee. He gave a quick wave and made his way over. "Now this is a good-looking bunch of ladies." He ruffled Violet's hair. "I heard you were hanging out with Nana and Aunt Mercedes while Mommy takes a nap."

"We're going to have a picnic at the park," Violet announced.

"A picnic? No fair."

"Do you want to come with us?"

"I have to work." Tony gave her a quick hug. "Maybe next time."

"We're here to borrow the stroller." Mercedes grabbed the handle and steered it toward the door. "Your child has some pretty powerful burps, bro."

Tony grinned. "I'm guessing you got the full Melody gas blast. Shelby has already talked to the doctor about her excessive burping. He doesn't seem concerned. She's gaining weight and digesting her formula well."

"Maybe she has a super digester," Mercedes said. "Thank goodness we haven't experienced what Violet calls the rooty toots."

"If you do, you're in for a real treat." Tony motioned to a customer who approached the counter. "I better get back to work. Have fun."

"I'm sure we will."

Cutting through the pawn shop, Mercedes, Melody and Violet waited on the sidewalk while Carlita ran to the other end of the block to grab their food from Ravello's.

It was a nearly picture-perfect day with comfortable temperatures and only a few fluffy clouds floating by in the sky. Because the summer season had recently ended, both vehicle traffic and pedestrian traffic were light.

Reaching the busy Bay Street intersection, they waited for the light to change before crossing to the other side. The Parrot House Restaurant's parking lot was only half full, similar to what Carlita had noticed when she picked up their food from Ravello's.

While Mercedes and the kids waited outside, Carlita ran upstairs to the apartment to grab Rambo. "Violet is here. Let's go for a walk."

The pup, who had been snoozing in his doggie bed, promptly scrambled to his feet when he heard Violet's name. He bolted past her, ran down the steps, and flew out of the building.

Carlita caught up with Rambo, who was already at Violet's side, his tail wagging fast and furious. "You should've seen him. As soon as he heard Violet's name, he took off like a rocket."

"And he ran right to her," Mercedes said. "Before we know it, Melody will be tottering around, chasing after him."

"I can't wait." Carlita could feel a tug of emotion as she watched the pup and her granddaughter reunite. An inkling of sadness was mingled in...sad about the fact she was so far away from Noel,

Paulie, Gracie, and little Vinny, her other grandchildren. "One of these days, we need to get the rest of the family down here."

"Tony's got some extra room now, thanks to you."

"Nana gave us another house."

Carlita smiled. "I gave you some extra space and your own bedroom."

"Because you're the best Nana in the whole wide world." Violet grabbed hold of her hand and leaned in. "I love you," she whispered.

Carlita knelt next to her. "And I love you." Feeling emotional, she blinked back the tears and sucked in a breath. "Shall we stop by to say hello to the Waving Girl?"

"The Waving Girl. The Waving Girl," Violet chanted. "Let's go, Rambo!"

Because the restaurant and Pete and Carlita's apartment were only a quick jaunt away from the popular park, they reached the Savannah River in no time.

"Help Nana find the perfect picnic spot," Carlita said.

"I will." Violet tromped down the small incline. She walked in circles and returned to where they stood waiting. "Over here."

Mercedes and Carlita, with Melody content in her stroller, followed the young girl to a grassy knoll away from other park visitors, yet only steps from the river.

"I brought a blanket." Mercedes removed a plaid blanket from the bag and spread it out on the grass. "What's for lunch?"

"I'm not sure. I told Arnie we were going on a picnic with Violet and he asked if he could surprise us."

"As long as it's not spinach and sardines." Violet wrinkled her nose.

"I'm sure he didn't pack either of those."

Baby Melody started to fuss. "I think it might be time for a bottle."

Carlita removed it from the travel bag, popped the top, and began feeding her. The baby hungrily sucked down the formula, barely stopping long enough to take a breath. "No wonder she has a lot of gas. She eats very fast."

"Don't take it away," Violet warned.

It was too late. Thinking she was gulping it down too quickly, Carlita pulled it out of her mouth, breaking the suction.

Melody started wailing loudly, her tiny fists and feet flailing as she demanded her bottle back.

"She has a healthy set of lungs," Mercedes said.

A couple walked by, slowing when the baby's screams grew even louder.

"She's hungry." Carlita shrugged.

The woman nodded. They kept walking, but she glanced over her shoulder when Melody ramped up her displeasure at not being fed.

"You better give it back," Violet sighed. "She won't stop until you do."

Carlita promptly placed the bottle back in her mouth and she grew quiet. "We might as well wait until she finishes eating."

"She's fast, Nana."

"I bet she is."

Melody polished off the bottle. Carlita promptly removed her from the stroller and began patting her back. They walked in circles with the baby burping once, twice, three times in a row.

She started to doze off. Carlita carefully placed her inside the stroller and tucked the blankets around her. "The little sweetheart was hungry and now it's naptime."

Mercedes clapped her hands. "We should eat before round two of the 'burpfest' begins," she joked.

"You're probably right." Carlita removed the bags of food and placed them on the edge of the blanket. She plucked her purse from the storage area and set it by her side. Her cell phone slid out and Carlita noticed she'd missed several texts and calls. "Someone has been trying to get ahold of me."

She tapped the screen. Elvira's number popped up. "It's Elvira. I'll call her after we eat." Carlita started to turn it off when another text popped up from her former neighbor. *Hey, Carlita. It's me. Please call me right away.*

Chapter 12

"Great," Carlita groaned. "Elvira called several times and sent two urgent texts. I better find out what's going on."

"Can it wait until after we eat?" Mercedes asked.

"You're right. Why ruin a perfectly good meal?" She started to put her phone away.

Ting.

"There she is again." Carlita sighed heavily. "I might as well answer it. If not, she's going to keep pestering me."

"I'm hungry," Violet pouted.

"Here. Have a cracker." Mercedes pulled a pack of snack crackers from the bag and handed it to her.

Carlita pressed the answer button. "Hello, Elvira."

"Hey, Carlita. Why didn't you call me back?"

"Which time? The first, second, third or fourth time?"

"I only called three times. Well, I guess this would be my fourth. What's going on down there?"

"What do you mean?"

"Dernice sent me some pictures of the damage to my ductwork. She said someone broke in."

"It was after last night's fundraiser." Carlita started to explain what had happened.

Elvira cut her off. "I already heard. So, who was it?"

"We don't know. From what we can tell, two people were involved. They attended the fundraiser and purchased a raffle ticket for Colby's Corner Store."

"And then they broke into the place because they didn't win?" Elvira asked incredulously.

"Maybe. I mean, I suppose anything is possible. I've already talked to Ken. They took some snacks, supplements and energy drinks."

"But no cash or other goods?"

"Nope."

"It doesn't make sense. What did they get from the pawn shop?"

"Nothing. They busted out the upstairs window to nowhere."

"Whoever it is doesn't sound very bright," Elvira scoffed. "Dernice said they didn't take anything from my place either. I have a theory."

"About the burglary?"

"Yeah. The only reason my place was hit is because it's right next door to your pawn shop."

"That's a pretty flimsy theory," Carlita said. "I was thinking more along the lines of you bragging to the wrong people about your quest for riches and gold, which made you a target."

"Not as flimsy as blaming it on me," Elvira blustered. "I can tell you one thing. If they get caught, they're going to pay for the damage to my place."

"The burglar didn't damage the ductwork." Carlita knew as soon as the words were out of her mouth she'd made a mistake…and inadvertently thrown Dernice under the bus.

"What do you mean? They tore it apart."

"I…uh. Not quite."

"Hold up. If they weren't the ones who damaged my property who was it? Did you try crawling in there?"

"It wasn't me." Carlita briefly closed her eyes. "I'm sorry I said anything."

"Dernice. Dernice was the one who got stuck in the ductwork and had to be cut out. I knew it. She's a terrible liar."

"Your sister was only trying to help. The damage isn't that bad. I'm sure it can easily be repaired."

"She's going to get an earful," Elvira ranted. "I've only been gone for a couple of days and the place is already falling apart."

"It's not falling apart. Seriously, you should rethink chewing Dernice out. She was only trying to retrieve a potential clue. Besides, do you think it's wise to get onto her while you're on the other side of the country and she's running things?"

Carlita could hear light tapping on the other end of the line.

"No," Elvira finally said. "I can't have her walking off the job now."

"Like I said, it's not too bad, and she was only trying to help."

"Yeah." Elvira's voice grew calmer. "Dernice can be a little impulsive at times, but she has a good heart."

"Like someone else I know," Carlita teased.

"We're definitely related."

"So, how's it going up there?"

"Alaska is pretty. I'm getting settled in. The accommodations leave a lot to be desired." Elvira lowered her voice. "Believe me, I'm not complaining. The head guy is a sexy hunk."

"You find him attractive, I take it?"

She made a popping sound with her lips. "He's hot in a rugged sort of way."

"What about Sharky?"

"What about him?"

"Does he know you're there?"

"I've been sending him a few clues. I think he's figuring it out."

"Well...good luck."

"Thanks."

Carlita started to say goodbye. Elvira stopped her. "Hey."

"What?"

"Can you keep an eye on the place? I wouldn't be surprised if these clowns show up again and actually take something this time."

"The Walton Square community has been notified. There will be lots of eyes and ears on the lookout."

"Cool." Elvira's voice grew muffled. "I gotta go. Ciao."

"Do you…" It was too late. Elvira had hung up.

Mercedes watched her mother slide her cell phone back into her purse. "How is she?"

"Wound up tighter than a top. I sure hope she knows what she's doing in Alaska."

"Elvira has officially been let loose in the last frontier." Mercedes rolled her eyes. "Hopefully, she behaves herself."

The same uneasy feeling Carlita had gotten when she dropped Elvira off at the airport returned. Something told her the woman would come home with some hair-raising tales to share—and none of them would involve interactions with Alaska's wildlife.

141

Chapter 13

Carlita reached into the restaurant's to-go bag and removed the container marked "Violet." "This is for you."

"Thanks, Nana." She carefully set it on her lap.

"You're welcome." She removed the second container and handed it to Mercedes. "This is for you, and this last one must be mine."

Along with the food was a plastic bag filled with packets of parmesan cheese, napkins and plastic cutlery. "Arnie remembered everything."

Violet opened the lid, grabbed the slice of garlic bread sitting on top, and took a big bite. "Yummy."

Carlita opened the lid on her lunch. The tantalizing aroma of garlic mingled with fresh rosemary wafted out. Her mouth watered. "This looks fabulous."

Mercedes smacked her lips. "Arnie is the best. He packed a favorite dish of mine—smoky red pepper pasta."

"Peppers." Violet, displaying a smidgen of drama, clutched her throat. "I don't like peppers."

Carlita chuckled. "They're not hot. Besides, red peppers are good for you."

The young girl crossed her arms, a suspicious look on her face. "But they're red. I don't like red food."

"You like spaghetti and meatballs," Mercedes said. "In fact, it's your favorite dish."

"I love s'getti and meatballs."

Mercedes nudged her arm. "Maybe you'll love red peppers as much as you love spaghetti and meatballs."

"I won't."

"At least try it," her grandmother said.

Violet shook her head, a stubborn gleam in her eye.

"If you don't try it, you can't have dessert."

"What's for dessert?"

Carlita peeked inside the bag. "Cookies with sprinkles."

"Cookies." Violet scrambled across the blanket. "Sprinkle cookies are my favorite."

"Then I guess you'll try the pasta."

"Okay. But only a little in case it makes my stomach hurt," the child bargained.

"It's a deal. Try a bite. If you don't like it, then you don't have to eat it."

Violet grabbed a fork and dug in.

Carlita waved her cutlery packet in her daughter's direction. "Spoiled rotten. Arnie spoils you rotten."

"Because I always volunteer to cover shifts when he's short-staffed."

"It's true. You're a hard worker." Carlita shot Violet a furtive side glance. She was eating the pasta...not only eating it, but taking big bites.

Mercedes caught her mother's eye and winked.

While they feasted, Violet shared stories about school and some of her friends. It seemed as if, right before Carlita's eyes, the young girl had grown into a thoughtful and mature little lady.

In a small way, it made her sad to think that soon Violet would be too busy for picnics with her grandmother and aunt. She hoped not. The Garlucci and now Garlucci-Taylor families were a close-knit group.

Violet and Melody were part of the next generation. Carlita's most fervent desire was to pass her businesses, all she had worked so hard to create, to her children so they could continue the family legacy long after she was gone.

The family legacy, at least as far as Tony was concerned. Paulie, the mayor of Clifton Falls, a small town about an hour north of New York City, might never move to Savannah. Regardless, he was in a good place, had a good job, and a loving family. If he stayed there for the rest of his life, Carlita would be content.

Her oldest son, Vinnie, was an entirely different story. On her husband's deathbed, she'd promised to get their sons out of "the family," aka the mob. The mafia. Organized crime in Queens, New York.

She'd kept her promise as far as Tony was concerned and had even been successful in helping Luigi Baruzzo, a former bodyguard for the Castellini family, break free.

Vinnie, unfortunately, was not only deeply involved in the family, but he was also married to the daughter of the deceased Vito Castellini, head of the mafia. Vinnie, his wife Brittney and their young son lived in New Jersey, where he managed one of the "family" casinos.

Although it was rarely discussed, she'd caught snippets of conversations that Brittney wanted out, wanted to move away to a more stable and less violent environment to raise their child. Which meant there was still hope, at least in Carlita's mind, that she could keep her promise.

If they eventually left, she believed Vinnie Senior could finally rest in peace, knowing his sons and grandchildren were safe. Carlita hoped his dying wish wouldn't end up being hers as well. Only time would tell.

"I ate every bite." Violet proudly showed her grandmother the empty container.

"I guess the red peppers weren't so bad after all."

"They tasted like sauce."

"Would you eat the pasta again?"

Violet nodded. "But maybe next time we can have s'getti."

"Maybe." Carlita plucked the packet of cookies from the bag and handed it to her.

She peeled back the plastic. Careful not to lose any of the sprinkles, she handed a cookie to her aunt. "One for Aunt Mercedes." She gave the second cookie to Carlita. "One for Nana and one for me."

"Thank you." Carlita finished her pasta and bit into the cookie. "I've never been a huge fan of sugar cookies, but this is tasty."

"The buttery treat melts in your mouth," Mercedes mumbled. "I'm stuffed."

"We'll need to walk this off."

Rambo, who had been sniffing around, looking for treats, plopped down in front of Carlita, guilting her with a sad puppy dog look. "Sorry, buddy. I don't think there's anything you can eat."

"Hang on." Mercedes tipped the paper bag over. A small serving of grilled chicken fell onto the blanket. "Arnie didn't forget Rambo."

"I'll give Rambo his treats." Violet peeled the lid off the container and began feeding the pup the pieces. "Can we go to the water when we're done?"

"Of course." Carlita began gathering up the containers and trash. She accidentally bumped the side of the stroller.

Melody started to stir. She blinked a few times and began kicking her feet.

"Someone is awake." Carlita shoved the bag of trash in the bin beneath the stroller and carefully lifted her tiny granddaughter out.

The baby's left hand jerked back and forth, as if trying to touch her grandmother's face. Carlita leaned in, pressing the chubby fist to her cheek. "There's our little ray of sunshine. Did you have a nice nap?"

Violet hopped over the blanket and chased after Rambo, who had gotten his second wind after devouring his treat. He collided with the back of the stroller. It began rolling.

Mercedes lunged forward, attempting to grab it. The stroller picked up speed and rolled down the hill, heading straight toward the sidewalk.

Carlita tightened her grip on the baby, watching in horror as her daughter chased after the runaway buggy. Out of the corner of her eye, she spotted a bicyclist cruising toward it on a direct collision course.

"Heads up!" Mercedes tried to warn the biker. It was too late. He collided with the stroller. For a second, Carlita was certain he was going to crash, but somehow he kept his balance. The baby's buggy bounced off the concrete post and toppled onto its side.

The man on the bike came to a full stop. He hopped off and ran over to the stroller. "Oh my gosh. I'm sorry. I didn't see it coming toward me." He turned it upright, visibly relieved to discover it was empty.

Carlita, with Violet by her side and Melody in her arms, hurried down the incline. "Thank God I was holding the baby." She shuddered, literally sick to her stomach at the thought that her granddaughter had been in the stroller only seconds earlier and could easily have been inside when it took off down the hill. "We must have forgotten to lock the wheels."

"It's too late now." Mercedes frowned, tapping the side of the bent frame. "I don't know if this can be fixed."

Carlita shifted the baby to her other hip. "The wheel is crooked."

Her daughter steered it forward. The wheel wobbled and pulled hard to the right. "Great. I don't think this is gonna work."

"Do you want me to try bending it back?" the biker offered.

"If you don't mind."

"Not at all."

The women and Violet hovered off to the side, watching as the man tried bending the bar connected to the wheel. He had limited success.

"Thank you." Mercedes tried pushing it again. Although it was better, it made a grinding noise and still wobbled to the right.

"I'm sorry about the stroller," he apologized.

"It's not your fault. Thank you for trying to fix it." Carlita waited until he rode off. "I guess we'll have to walk home."

The trio, with Rambo by their side, trekked back up the hill with Mercedes dragging the stroller behind her. "Let's stop by the house to get the car," Carlita said.

Ting...ting...ting...ting-a-ling.

"The trolley." Violet hopped up and down. "Can we take the trolley, Nana?"

"That's a great idea." Carlita handed the baby to Mercedes. She stepped onto the edge of the street and flagged down her friend Claryce, "Reese" Magillicuddy, who ran the Walton Square / Bay Street trolley route.

Reese waved back and began applying the brakes. "Hold on, folks. We're making an emergency stop." She eased onto the edge near the curb and turned the trolley's flashers on. "Hey, Carlita."

"Hey, Reese. Melody's stroller crashed, and the wheel got bent."

Mercedes dragged it closer. "It's gonna need a serious wheel alignment."

"We have too much stuff," Violet announced.

"There's plenty of room for it right behind my seat. I must warn you we'll be looping around which means you'll be riding my entire route."

"Gladly. Thank you, Reese. You're a lifesaver."

"I do have a knack for being in the right place at the right time."

"Yes, you do." Carlita slipped into an empty seat, making way for Mercedes, who was dragging the stroller up the trolley steps. "Reese to the rescue."

"Reese to the rescue." Violet giggled, repeating her aunt's phrase. "Can we stop for ice cream?"

Chapter 14

As soon as they were seated, Reese pulled back onto the street. "Thanks for inviting me to Steve's fundraiser. I ran into so many people I haven't seen in ages. It was like a reunion."

"A great group of locals coming together to help one of their own. And thank you for persuading your boss to let us raffle off a month of free rides on the trolley," Carlita said. "I'm sure it was popular."

"It was," Mercedes said. "Actually, all of them were awesome raffle goodies."

"Too bad it ended on a grim note."

Reese shot Carlita a puzzled look in the rearview mirror. "Ended on a grim note? What happened?"

"Two burglars tried breaking into the pawn shop. The same pair broke into Elvira's business. They also stole some stuff from Colby's Corner Store."

"Last night?"

"Yeah. During the fundraiser or right after it ended."

"That's odd and sort of interesting," Reese said.

"Why?"

"Because I ran into Russell Sterling at the fundraiser. He mentioned his place had been broken into a few weeks ago."

Carlita's heart skipped a beat. "No kidding. Did they steal anything?"

"No, but they messed the place up pretty good. He said he caught them on his surveillance camera." Reese described the burglars to a "t." "Dark clothes, athletic yet klutzy. He said they somehow managed to disable his alarm system."

"So maybe they're not as bumbling as they appear to be." Mercedes and her mother exchanged a quick glance. "This sounds like the same two."

"Sterling," Carlita said. "Why does his name sound familiar?"

"Russell Sterling owns Sterling Automotive Group. I'm sure you've seen his commercials."

"You're right. I have. I guess we never met," Carlita said.

"I'm not sure how Steve knows him. Or maybe he doesn't. Maybe someone else invited him or told him about the event," Reese said.

The conversation paused when they reached their next stop. Several riders got off while a few more boarded. In between stops, they threw out theories about who might be behind the break-ins. Carlita's gut told her Sterling's incident could be related to theirs, but how?

The ride flew by, and before they knew it, they were back in Walton Square. It took a little finagling to gather up all of their stuff and drag the damaged stroller down the steps.

"Call Tony and tell him to come help," Mercedes said.

"Good idea." Carlita dialed her son's cell phone number and waved goodbye to Reese as the trolley rumbled off.

"Hey, Ma."

"Hey, Son. We had a little accident during our picnic. We're near the trolley stop. Can you come help?"

"Is everyone okay?"

"We're fine but we need a hand carrying the stuff."

"I'm on my way." Tony hurried out of the building and caught up with them. "What happened?"

"Rambo bumped the stroller. We forgot to lock the wheels. It took off down the hill, hit a cement post and the frame got bent." Carlita tightened her grip on the baby. "Thank goodness I was holding Melody when it happened."

"Unfortunately, we're not sure if it can be fixed," Mercedes said.

Tony grabbed the handle and tested it out. "Yeah. I can fix it. I forgot to mention the stroller is an easy glide."

"Almost too easy." Carlita swiped at her forehead. "We were on our way back when we ran into Reese and the trolley. She gave us a ride."

"Thanks for taking the girls," Tony said. "Shelby stopped by the pawn shop a few minutes ago. She took a nap, ran an errand, and is back home now."

"We'll drop Melody and Violet off."

Tony picked up the damaged stroller. "Do you need help?"

"Thanks, but I think we can handle it."

Taking the shortcut along the side of the pawn shop, Carlita and Melody waited outside while

Violet and Mercedes went upstairs to the apartment to pack Violet's art supplies and the baby's bag.

They returned in a flash and made their way to the family's home at the other end of the alley. Shelby appeared moments later, looking rested and relaxed. "I was getting ready to send you a text that I was up from my nap and home."

"We ran into Tony on our way here." Carlita told her about the runaway stroller. "I'm sorry to say it will need some repairs."

"It's an easy glide," Shelby said. "It's almost too easy of a glide. You need to make sure you lock the wheels when you're stopped."

"Thank goodness I had the baby when Rambo bumped it."

The women chatted for a few minutes, with Shelby thanking them multiple times for offering to watch the children.

Carlita made her promise to let her know the next time she needed a break before she and Mercedes backtracked to her apartment.

"I don't know about you, but those kids wore me out," Mercedes sighed.

"Violet is a busy bee. I'm glad we could help Shelby and give both girls some undivided attention. And even got some fresh air, isn't that right, Rambo?" Carlita playfully fluffed her pup's ears.

"What do you think about what Reese said about the Sterling guy?"

"I'm not sure. I guess it wouldn't hurt to talk to Steve to find out how he knows him." Carlita lingered when they reached the alley's rear entrance. "Maybe I'll swing by there again and ask him about it."

Mercedes reached for the doorknob. Her mother stopped her. "I've been meaning to ask...how is it going?"

"How's what going?"

"You and Sam. The romantic getaway to Hilton Head."

Sam had tracked Mercedes down during a recent community service punishment, handed down by a local judge. She'd spent the day picking up trash in downtown Savannah. He had not only tracked her down but also humiliated her in front of his tour group.

Quickly realizing the error of his ways, he sent her a beautiful bouquet of roses and booked a romantic getaway at an upscale resort in nearby Hilton Head. It was a much-needed break for the couple and when they returned, they both seemed to have enjoyed the trip.

Although Carlita had been dying to know how it went, yet not wanting to pry, she decided to wait for Mercedes to bring it up. A few weeks had already passed and yet neither had uttered a peep about it.

Mercedes shrugged. "It was nice."

"Nice to get away? Nice to spend time alone with Sam? Nice to go somewhere new?"

"All the above."

"I understand," Carlita said. "It's none of my business and you don't want to talk about it."

"There's nothing to talk about. We had a good time. Sam and I both work a lot. It was cool to just chill out and enjoy each other's company."

"So." Carlita gave her a thumbs up. "Everything is good between you two?"

"Status quo, Ma."

It was clear Mercedes wasn't in the mood to discuss the trip or her relationship and let it drop. "I love you, Mercedes. All I want is for you to be happy."

"I am happy." Her daughter impulsively hugged her. "Thanks for always being here for me. For all of us."

"You're welcome." Carlita hugged her back. "I think I'll run by Steve's to see what's up with this Sterling guy."

During the trek to the tattoo shop, she mulled over her conversation with Mercedes. Because Carlita was married and no longer residing under the same roof, she wasn't involved in her daughter's day-to-day life. Which was probably a good thing. Something told her that her youngest child was still finding her way, still testing out her wings and enjoying her freedom.

Carlita didn't blame her. In fact, if she was in her shoes, she would probably do the same thing. Sam was a good guy, a great guy, but was he the perfect person for Mercedes? Only time would tell.

Chapter 15

"I know Russell Sterling. He owns Sterling Automotive Group." Steve rubbed his thumb against his fingers. "He makes the big bucks. I'm sure you've seen his ads on television."

"Television ads? You're right. He's the fellow with the cheesy moustache and catchy slogan, 'Save big bucks and buy from us.'"

"That's the one. Russell's a decent guy who has had a string of bad luck, at least lately. He was here at the fundraiser."

"Reese mentioned two individuals who match the description of the burglars from last night also broke into his business."

"Really?" Steve arched his eyebrow. "I wonder if they're the same ones."

"It's possible. Do you think he would mind if I swung by and asked him about it?"

"I have no idea." Steve told her that it was a family-run business and Russell was in charge of the day-to-day operations. "Which means you have a pretty good chance of catching him at the dealership."

Carlita thanked him and she and Rambo returned home. As they passed by the parking lot, she noticed a shiny new SUV with New Jersey license plates parked off to the side. On closer inspection, she realized it was her oldest son, Vinnie's luxury SUV.

Picking up the pace, Carlita ran up the stairs, taking them two at a time. She reached the landing and heard voices along with the tinkle of laughter, a very distinctive laugh.

She flung the door open and found her son, daughter-in-law, and little Vin standing in the kitchen. The toddler spotted his grandmother. With arms wide open, he waddled across the floor and plowed into her.

Carlita scooped him up. Holding him tightly, she spun the little boy around. "What are you doing here?"

"We thought we would surprise you." Vinnie, grinning from ear to ear, sauntered over. "Pete said you missed us and invited us to come down for a few days."

Her husband, with a mischievous twinkle in his eye and looking pleased with himself for pulling off the surprise visit, folded his arms. "I almost spilled the beans last night."

Carlita set her grandson on the floor and hugged her son. "I have missed you all so much." She stepped back, holding him at arm's length. "You look good, like you're beefing up a bit. Have you put on a few pounds?"

"More than a few." Vinnie patted his gut. "I need to get back to the gym."

Brittney, looking as beautiful as always, as if she'd just stepped off the pages of *Vogue* magazine, tottered over in her high heels. "Pete invited us to stay here, but if it's too tight, we can always book a hotel room."

"Not on your life." Carlita gave Brittney a gentle hug, careful not to muss her meticulously coiffed blond locks. "You're as gorgeous as ever."

"Thanks." Brittney playfully patted her hair. "Vin upped my allowance for my beauty regimen. It takes some big bucks to keep all of this looking glam."

"You would be gorgeous with no makeup and your hair down, but if it makes you happy." Carlita motioned them back to the bar area. "Are you hungry? Can I get you something to drink?"

"We're fine, Ma," Vinnie said. "We grabbed a light snack on our way into town."

Little Vin let out a squeal and began chasing after Rambo, who led him around in circles.

"We were gonna fly, but decided it would take the same amount of time to drive," Vinnie said.

167

"Brittney has been champing at the bit to meet Melody."

"Mercedes and I took her and Violet on a picnic down at the park earlier so Shelby could get some rest."

The family wandered into the living room where Vinnie and Brittney took turns filling them in and catching up.

"How long can you stay?" Carlita finally asked.

"Unfortunately, like I said only for a couple of days." Vinnie motioned to Pete. "Pete promised you two would plan a trip to Jersey soon."

"We've talked about it."

"Why don't you caravan?" her son suggested. "Bring Mercedes, Sam, Tony, Shelby. Maybe even Elvira and her entourage. We'll invite Paulie and his gang to come down at the same time. I think even Luigi would be on board for a trip north."

Carlita playfully placed her hand on her son's forehead. "Did you say Elvira? Are you sure you're feeling all right?"

He chuckled, swatting it away. "On second thought, let me think about it."

"She's in Alaska."

"Alaska? What's in Alaska?"

"Gold mining," Pete said.

"Ah." Vinnie snapped his fingers. "I should've known. So...what else has been going on?"

"The pawn shop got broken into."

"At least the window got busted out," Pete elaborated.

"I discovered something interesting." Carlita filled Brittney and Vinnie in and then told Pete about Russell Sterling.

"I know Russ," Pete said. "He's been around for ages. So, his business was broken into as well?"

"According to what Reese said. I was thinking about running by there to find out what happened." Carlita glanced at her watch. "It's almost dinnertime. It can wait until tomorrow."

"I thought we could eat downstairs," Pete said. "I've already reserved the back room so we can enjoy a quiet meal."

"Quiet? We're talking about the Garluccis here." Carlita bounced on the tips of her toes and kissed her husband's cheek. "You're the best husband, the most thoughtful man. Thank you."

"You're welcome. It was worth the effort to see your face light up when you walked through the door," Pete said. "In fact, I let Mercedes and Tony in on the surprise. The rest of the family should be here any moment."

While the others headed to the restaurant, Carlita took a minute to freshen up. She thought about what Reese had said and the fact Sterling's place was also targeted.

The big questions were who and why. She pushed the troubling thought aside. It would have to wait. Tonight was all about family, and she wasn't going to waste another second worrying about the sloppy, amateur burglars.

Tomorrow was a new day. After a good night's sleep, she would be ready to dive in and hopefully start figuring out who it was.

Chapter 16

As soon as breakfast was over the next morning, Vinnie and his small family took off to do some sightseeing. Carlita and Pete hopped into his pickup for the short drive to the outskirts of town. "Sterling owns a couple of dealerships in the area. The one we're going to is the biggest of the bunch. I bought this truck from him, and if I remember correctly, his office was at this location."

They pulled into the lot and found an empty parking spot in front of the sprawling glass and brass building. There were cars, trucks, vans and SUVs everywhere, for as far as the eye could see.

Carlita let out a low whistle. "This place is huge."

"Like I said, his other lots are a little smaller." Pete climbed out and went around to the other side to hold the door for his wife. "Hopefully, Sterling is here and has time to chat with us."

Entering through the double doors, they stopped at the front desk. The receptionist directed them down a long, gleaming hallway to a row of offices. Behind the glass partitions, Carlita could see employees seated at their desks.

They made a sharp left and walked to the end, where they found another receptionist. A large black and gold sign affixed to the front of her modern semi-circular desk read, "Corporate Offices."

Pete approached the counter. "Good morning. My name is Pete Taylor. This is my wife, Carlita. We're wondering if Russell is around."

"Do you have an appointment with Mr. Sterling?"

"We do not."

"What is the reason for your visit?"

"It's a personal matter."

"He has a tight schedule and normally requires meeting appointments made in advance," she primly replied. "What did you say your name was?"

"Pete Taylor. We're local business owners. Mr. Sterling will recognize my name," he said.

"I'll check to see if he's available." The woman sprang from her chair and hurried off.

Carlita waited until she was gone. "Do you think he'll be curious enough to find out what the personal matter is?"

"Maybe." Pete rocked back on his heels. "I give it a fifty-fifty chance."

"I hope he does. If not, it's back to the drawing board," Carlita sighed. "And on to Plan B."

"Which is?"

"I have no idea." She noticed the woman coming toward them. "Here she comes," she whispered under her breath.

"Mr. Sterling has agreed to see you," the receptionist said. "But he only has a few minutes, so you'll need to make it quick."

"We will." Pete placed a light hand on Carlita's back as they followed the woman down the long hall to the office at the end.

Although the other offices were small squares with clear glass windows enabling those passing by to see inside, the CEO's windows sported privacy blinds, all of which were closed.

The woman gave the signal for them to enter. Carlita followed Pete inside the surprisingly spacious office. To the right was a seating area with oversized leather chairs and a matching sofa facing a floor-to-ceiling brick fireplace.

Windows on both sides of the fireplace offered views of a charming Savannah courtyard, filled with greenery and even a tiered, flowing fountain.

Sterling's desk, a large U-shaped modern style with the same glass and brass Carlita had noticed when they arrived, was opposite the cozy sitting area.

The style struck her as warm and inviting on one side as opposed to all business on the other. Seated behind the desk was a thin man with salt and pepper colored hair, poofy on top and slicked back on both sides. His thick moustache was the same salt and pepper shade.

He slowly stood. A flicker of recognition crossed his face when he saw the couple. Sterling strolled around the desk and extended his hand. "Pete Taylor. When Ginny said someone was here to see me and gave me your name, it didn't click." He grasped Pete's hand in a firm handshake. "How are you?"

"Doing good. Thank you for seeing us on such short notice." Pete motioned to Carlita. "This is my wife, Carlita."

"It's my pleasure to meet you." Sterling shook her hand and hesitated. "I believe I remember seeing you last night at Steve Winter's fundraiser, although we didn't officially meet. You own the authentic Italian restaurant in Walton Square."

"Ravello's Italian Eatery," Carlita said. "My daughter and I were co-hosting the event. As you can imagine, it was a little chaotic. It's nice to meet you as well."

"So...the receptionist said you were here to discuss a personal matter," he prompted.

"Our businesses were broken into after the fundraiser." Carlita told him what had happened. "I ran into Claryce Magillicuddy earlier. She mentioned you also recently had a break-in."

"I...uh. Yes." Sterling shoved his hands in his pockets. "The office was broken into. I filed a police report and haven't heard back."

"Obviously, you have surveillance cameras. Were you able to get a glimpse of who the vandals were?" Pete asked.

"I turned everything I had over to the investigators."

Carlita reached for her phone. "I have a recording of the two burglars who broke into my pawn shop, our corner store grocery, and my neighbor's business. Perhaps if you could take a quick look at what we have, you can tell us if they match your individuals."

Sterling's expression grew grim. "I don't want to see your video," he snapped. "Unless you're working with the investigators."

The way the man said it, Carlita knew he wasn't the least bit interested in figuring out if whoever broke into his car dealership were the same two who had burglarized the Walton Square businesses.

He pointedly tapped his watch. "At the risk of sounding rude, I have a conference call starting soon and need to get back to work."

Pete thanked him for his time. He remained silent until they had exited the office and returned to the truck. "That was an awkward conversation."

"Sterling wasn't at all interested in finding out if there might be a link between his break-in and ours," Carlita said. "As soon as he realized why we were there, he was in a big hurry to get us out."

"Maybe the authorities are close to figuring out who it is and Sterling knows it," Pete theorized.

"It's possible. If you don't mind, I would like to swing by the police department to see if we can get a copy of his police report."

"Your wish is my command."

Reaching the police station's parking lot, Carlita hopped out and caught up with her husband on the sidewalk. Although it had been some time since her last visit, it hadn't changed, projecting an overall gloominess.

The walls were a dull gray, almost the exact same color as the cement floors. Fluorescent lights ran the length of the ceiling. The lights did little to help brighten the drab interior.

The clerk behind the desk greeted them with the same level of enthusiasm the interior inspired. Carlita met the man's unhappy expression with a forced smile. "Good morning."

"Morning."

"My name is Carlita Taylor. Someone broke into my business the night before last. Not only my business, but two others in the neighborhood. We believe they may be linked to a similar break-in at Sterling Automotive Group and were wondering if we could get a copy of the police report."

"For your incident? Reports aren't released to the public for up to ten days."

"I understand. I would like a copy of the car dealership's police report."

"I'll have to charge you." The clerk rattled off what Carlita thought sounded like a reasonable fee.

"I'm okay with the fee."

He grabbed a pen and notepad. "What was the name again?"

"Sterling Automotive Group. I believe it happened two or three weeks ago."

"Wait here." Heaving a heavy sigh, the man shoved his chair back and tromped off.

"He's a cheerful fellow," Pete remarked.

"Who apparently loves his job," Carlita said sarcastically. "Life is too short to spend your days in a place that makes you miserable."

"I couldn't agree more." He playfully nudged her arm. "Speaking of life being too short, how is it going with booking our cruise vacation?"

"I'm thinking about working on it."

"Meaning you haven't started searching," Pete teased.

"Not yet. It's on my to do list, just not my today list."

"I guess I'll have to step up to the plate and plan it myself."

"Let's get our trip to New Jersey out of the way and then we can pick a date."

"It's a deal."

Their conversation ended when the clerk returned. He set a small stack of papers on the desk. "Your total is ten dollars and seventy cents."

"Ten dollars," Carlita gasped. "I thought you said it was only a couple of bucks."

"A couple dollars per page, plus tax."

"Highway robbery," she complained under her breath, as she fumbled with her wallet. Carlita reluctantly gave him the exact amount and took the papers. "I hope this is worth it."

"It would've been cheaper to go over there and get a copy from the other party."

"We already tried. He wasn't interested in talking." She thanked the man and followed her husband out of the police station. During the ride home, she skimmed over the papers. The first page was basic information about the incident. The date, the time, the responding officer.

She flipped to the next page and slid her glasses on, reading the handwritten notes about the burglary. Halfway down, a single sentence hit Carlita's radar. "Pete, I found something very interesting."

Chapter 17

"You found something interesting about Russell Sterling's burglary?"

"Yep." Carlita tapped the top of the police report. "This confirms what Reese mentioned. The perps tore Sterling's office apart."

"Maybe they thought he kept the good stuff in there."

"And they somehow figured out how to disarm his alarm system."

"Hmm...an inside job?"

"That's what I'm thinking. It was an inside job. What if Sterling found out he knew who the burglars were?" Carlita's mind whirled. "What if he figured it out and never turned them into the authorities?"

"Or it was Sterling himself," Pete said.

"But why would a successful business owner break into our businesses?"

"Unless the burglars were looking for something."

Carlita wrinkled her nose. "If it's the same people, and they were looking for something specific, why break into a grocery store? They're working on different ends of the spectrum. Goods versus information."

"You have a valid point. Elvira's place and Sterling's place are offices while the pawn shop and grocery store both stock goods. None of it makes sense."

"Nope." As soon as they got home, Pete took off to go check in with his restaurant manager.

After he left, Carlita placed the papers on the counter. She grabbed a pen and yellow pad and began jotting down notes about what she knew.

-Sterling attended the fundraiser.

-Sterling's business was also broken into.

-Sterling's burglars disarmed his alarm.

-Similar to Elvira's place, the burglars ransacked the office. Confirm with Dernice the office files were messed with.

-Raffle ticket found on Elvira's roof. From the fundraiser.

-When questioned, Sterling was reluctant to discuss the incident.

Carlita tracked down her cell phone and texted Dernice, asking if she was available to chat.

Wrapping up my gig. I'm heading back to the office to do some busywork.

Mind if I swing by?

Be my guest. I should be there in ten or less.

Thanks. See you soon.

While Carlita waited, she read Sterling's police report word for word and line by line. The more she read, the more convinced she was that his burglary was an inside job. But how was it linked to the

Walton Square break-ins and theft at Colby's Corner Store?

At the ten-minute mark, Carlita gathered up the papers and ran downstairs. She hopped in her car and drove straight over to Elvira's place.

Reaching the parking lot, she found Dernice standing in front of Elvira's work van. Vinnie stood nearby, smoking a cigarette. "Hey, Ma."

"Hey, Son. Where's Brittney and little Vin?"

"Visiting with Shelby and Violet. I came out to have a smoke and ran into Dernice."

"I was telling him Elvira is gonna be bummed she missed seeing him." Dernice snapped her fingers. "Can you do me a huge favor?"

"What?"

"Take a picture of Vinnie and me."

Carlita tilted her head. "You want me to take a picture of you and my son?"

"For Elvira."

To describe Elvira as having a crush on Carlita's son might be a slight understatement. The woman was madly in love with Vinnie. Carlita might be a little biased, but she thought all of her sons were good-looking guys, like their father had been.

But Vinnie had a little something extra. Maybe it was his swagger or the way he looked at the ladies that made them swoon. Or it could be his "bad boy" image attracted them. Whatever it was, Elvira was somewhat obsessed, at least as far as he was concerned.

He took a final drag off his cigarette and tossed the butt on the ground. "You two sure like to mess with each other."

"Hand me the phone."

"Would it be too much trouble for us to look like we're…"

"Cozy?" Vinnie suggested.

"Yeah. Cozy."

"Not at all." Graciously accommodating Dernice's request, Vinnie placed his arm around her shoulders. She leaned in with a look of pure delight on her face.

Carlita snapped several pictures and handed the phone back. "I took a few."

"Thanks. Man, is she gonna be kicking herself," Dernice cackled. "This is great. Thanks, Vinnie."

"You're welcome." He excused himself and headed back inside Tony and Shelby's apartment.

"Poor Elvira is missing out all the way around." Carlita waved the file folder she was holding in the air. "I have some interesting information, possibly linking the Walton Square burglaries to another recent incident."

"What is it?"

"Before I show you, I got to thinking about the break-in here at Elvira's. You mentioned it looked as if maybe some of your files or filing cabinets had been tampered with."

189

"They were. At first, I thought an employee had been in a hurry and left them messed up, but after checking around, nobody claims to have done it."

"Unless they didn't want to admit to making a mess," Carlita said.

"Yeah. You wouldn't know it by the looks of her van, but Elvira is a stickler for being tidy, at least as far as the business is concerned. The employees know me. They know I wouldn't get onto them about it. All the staff has heard about the burglary and would tell me if it had been one of them."

"So, we're back to the theory maybe the burglars were digging around looking for something."

"They wasted their time. Elvira locks up high-profile or potentially problematic cases for obvious reasons. The other burglary you mentioned, did they happen to have their office trashed?"

"Yes. They broke into the building, somehow disarmed the alarm and targeted the owner's office," Carlita said. "Pete and I went by there a little while ago to ask the guy about it. He was...shall we say...less than cooperative."

"Less than cooperative?"

"I offered to show him our surveillance footage of the burglars breaking in. He said something along the lines of unless we were investigators, he wasn't interested."

"Weird." Dernice frowned. "Did he say if they took anything of value, like cash on hand?"

"No." Carlita handed the report to Dernice. "Here's a copy of the police report."

Dernice flipped the folder open and studied the top sheet. Her eyes grew round as saucers. "Russell Sterling's business was broken into?" She rattled off the date. "We need to track down Elvira."

"Why?"

"Because Sterling hired EC Investigative Services not long ago to look into discrepancies in his company's books."

Chapter 18

Carlita stared at Dernice. "Russell Sterling hired Elvira to look into his company's finances?"

"Not technically," Dernice said. "He hired her to have someone. That someone was me—to slide in undercover and try to determine why his books weren't balancing. Sterling basically suspected an employee was stealing."

"Were you able to get to the bottom of it?"

"Yep. It was a little tricky. He employs a lot of family members, which is why he needed someone from the outside to kind of…" Dernice made a smooth line with her hand. "…swoop in and try to figure out what was going on."

"Who was it?" Carlita held her breath.

"I don't know. I was able to narrow it down to employee identification numbers but didn't hang around long enough to find out who it was." Dernice went into a technical explanation about how she figured out the money discrepancies occurred at the same time every week. Not large amounts, but enough so that eventually it became a significant sum. "Sterling is el cheapo. He uses the old punch a card time clock which helped me track down the thieves' ID numbers."

"So, it was an inside job?"

"Most definitely," Dernice said.

Carlita started to pace, struggling to put the pieces together. "But why break into the pawn shop and Colby's Corner Store?"

"It seems random. I mean, why would Sterling's thieves come over here to Walton Square?"

"Because they found out he hired Elvira's company and were desperate to get their hands on the evidence before he did, so they broke in. They didn't try very hard to get into the pawn shop. Maybe they broke into Colby's because they were hungry." Carlita blinked rapidly. "Unless it was Sterling. He left the fundraiser and then broke into our businesses."

She immediately dismissed the idea. "He's too tall. The burglars were both shorter than he is."

"Sterling was at the fundraiser? I never saw him. Of course, I showed up late to the party because I had to work," Dernice said.

"He must have been gone by then."

"Let me finish going over the report." Dernice grew quiet, poring over the information. "This sounds exactly like what happened to us."

"Let's go with the theory whoever they were knew about the investigation and were desperate to get their hands on the report, not knowing Elvira had already turned it over to Russell Sterling."

"It's possible, especially if it was a family member. Too bad we don't have access to Elvira's dark web.

We could hack into Sterling's site and figure out who it was."

"Where is Elvira's report?"

"Locked in the safe." Dernice pulled a set of keys from her pocket. "I have the combination. By the way, she's ticked about the damaged ductwork. Maybe if we tell her we're hot on the trail of whoever broke in, she'll give us access to her backdoor search engine."

"It's worth a shot." Carlita took the folder from her and tucked it inside her purse. "I'll try not to take much of your time."

"Don't worry about it." Dernice patted the side of the EC Investigative Services van. "Hop in."

"To ride halfway around the block?"

"Sure. I meant to park out front, but when I saw Vinnie, I couldn't resist and had to stop to say hello. Not only is your son good looking, but he has the fancy word. It starts with a 'c'".

"Charm?"

"No."

"Come-hither looks?"

"No, but you're close." Dernice snapped her fingers. "He has charisma. You know, the vibe that makes you tingle inside."

"Vinnie has had more than his share of women chase after him." Carlita started to open the passenger door and hesitated. "Does Elvira know you're driving her van?"

"Nope." Dernice held a finger to her lips. "Please don't mention it to her. She'll throw a fit. I'm gonna have this thing professionally cleaned and detailed before she gets back. Hop in, but be careful. It's a deathtrap, not to mention gross."

Carlita cautiously removed several containers from the passenger seat and set them on the floor. She slid onto the seat and reached for the door handle, instantly regretting touching it. "There's something sticky on the door handle."

"It's probably guava juice. Elvira's been binging on it lately. She heard it has a lot of fiber."

"Is she lacking fiber?" Carlita waved dismissively. "Never mind. I don't want to know."

"Personally, I find it's too sweet, but she seems to dig it." Dernice fired up the engine. She stomped on the gas and raced to the corner before making a sharp right. One more hard right and they reached the front of the building.

"That was quick."

"The quicker, the better. Did you notice the rancid smell?"

"It smells like Elvira's natto," Carlita said. "It has a very distinct odor."

Dernice made a gagging sound. "It's disgusting."

"I have to admit, I'm not a fan either." Grabbing her purse, Carlita hopped out and followed the woman inside.

"Spy," Elvira's parrot squawked. "Carlita spy. Where's Elvira?"

"In Alaska," Dernice said. "Elvira is in Alaska."

"Snitchy Snitch Alaska."

"I wish you were in Alaska," Dernice sighed.

"If you need a break while Elvira is gone, Gunner would love to have her over for a visit."

"Thanks for the offer. Give me a few more days, when Snitch is driving me crazy and I'll be begging you to take her."

"Ditzy Dernice."

Carlita covered her mouth to hide her smile. "She learned a new phrase."

"Unfortunately. I have no idea why my sister is so attached to this bird. If it was me, I would give her the boot."

"Booty boot," Snitch said.

"We've heard enough. I'm relocating you." Dernice carried the bird and her cage out of the room and returned empty-handed. "Where were we?"

"Getting ready to look at Elvira's report on Sterling Automotive Group."

"Right. I'll need to get it from the safe." She left again and reappeared, waving a manila file folder in the air. "Elvira is gonna have a cow when she finds out I have the code to the safe. She's the only person who is supposed to know it."

"How did you find out what it was?"

"Easy. It's her birth date plus her favorite number. It took me a few tries, but I figured it out."

"I hope this won't get you into any trouble." Carlita frowned.

"Nah. If Elvira finds out, she'll get over it." Dernice pulled a chair around to the back side of the desk and opened the folder. Going page by page, she filled Carlita in on the investigation and how she'd infiltrated the company, befriended the employees and used the information to figure out how the thieves were stealing.

"Like I said, most of the office workers, a good number of the sales staff, and even the peeps who work in service are related to Russell Sterling. Based on what you told me and how reluctant he was to talk about it, something tells me he knows who broke into his business."

Dernice sent a text to her sister, asking her to call. While they waited, they went over the police report. Finally, the phone rang.

"Hey, Elvira."

"Hey, Dernice. How's it going? Did you get a quote to repair the ductwork you damaged?"

"I'm getting several quotes. By the way, Carlita is here with me. I have you on speaker." Dernice filled her sister in on what they had found. "Do you remember the Sterling Automotive Group investigation?"

"Sure. How could I forget? I hope Sterling fired the employees who were stealing from him."

"His place got broken into a couple of weeks ago," Carlita said.

"Seriously? Who was it?"

"I don't know. I stopped by the police department and got a copy of the report. It sounds eerily similar to what happened here at Walton Square. Pete and I went by there earlier today. Sterling doesn't want to talk about it."

"Why not?" Elvira asked.

"My guess is the same people who stole from Sterling and burglarized his place broke into your office."

"Ah. Maybe he knows who it was. Maybe it was a family member. He's trying to cover for his family and has no plans to turn them in," Elvira said.

"I was thinking the same thing. He somehow knows or suspects they could be behind what happened to us and, for whatever reason, is protecting them," Carlita said.

"We have the employee numbers," Elvira said. "The file is locked away in the safe."

Dernice tapped the top of the stack of papers. "Got it right here."

"The Sterling file?"

"Yep."

"How did you get in the safe?" Elvira demanded.

"I figured out the code."

"Great. Now I'll have to change it," she grumbled.

"We need something else," Carlita said. "Dernice seems to think if we can access your dark web website, we can track down the Sterling Automotive Group's employee badge numbers and figure out who it was that broke into his place and most likely broke in here."

"Before we delve any deeper into this, why did they bust the pawn shop window and go rummaging around in Colby's Corner Store?"

"Maybe to throw investigators off. I don't think they had any intention of stealing from the pawn shop. The window they broke was the window to nowhere."

"But they stole stuff from Colby's place."

"Colby's Corner Store was a theft of convenience, if you ask me," Carlita said. "So...will you help us get into Sterling's site?"

Loud tapping ensued on the other end. "I would be breaking my promise to Sharky."

"Then don't tell us how to access his dark web," Dernice said. "You have other sites."

"True." Elvira grew quiet...so quiet Carlita thought they'd been disconnected. "Hello?"

"I'm here. Okay. Fine, but only this once. Pinky swear that you won't write down any of the login information."

"I swear," Dernice said.

"Ditto," Carlita said.

"No. Say it. Say you swear."

Carlita rolled her eyes. "I swear. I won't write your login information down."

"Good." Elvira rattled off the dark web website's address, her username and password.

While she talked, Dernice tapped the keys. "We're in. Now what?"

"Must I do everything for you?"

Dernice mimicked a yapping sound with her hand and pointed at the phone. "Yes, please."

Elvira directed her sister through the screens. In less than two minutes, they were in Sterling's company files. "Go to the identification screen, type in the employee identification number and press enter."

Dernice did as she instructed. She typed in the number and hit enter. Up popped an employee file. Her jaw dropped. "Good gravy. No wonder Russell Sterling doesn't want the cops linking these burglaries together."

Chapter 19

Carlita squinted her eyes. "Who is it?"

"Lindsay Sterling, Russell Sterling's daughter."

"What about the other employee identification number?" Elvira asked.

"I'm working on it." Dernice's fingers flew over the keys. "Just as I thought. The other identification belongs to Tracy Sterling, Russell's youngest daughter."

"What do they look like?" Carlita asked.

"One was a little chunky. The other, Tracy, was thin and athletic."

"Athletic enough to scale the side of a building?"

Dernice thought about it for a minute. "Probably."

Elvira let out a loud whistle. "This is all making sense. Tracy and Lindsay figured out their father was onto them about cooking the books and siphoning money. If I had to guess, Sterling got the report and planned to confront them."

"Before he did, they found out about the fundraiser. They knew Russell was attending, knew it was here in Walton Square, so they decided it was the perfect opportunity to break into your business to steal whatever evidence you may have had," Carlita said.

"Not knowing the cat was already out of the bag," Elvira said. "Or that the 'cat burglars' were out of the bag seeing how they like climbing buildings, or at least one of them does."

"Very funny." Dernice tugged on her blouse. "I mean, it makes sense. My guess is they also targeted Savannah Swag and Colby's Corner Store to make it appear random."

"The big question is...how can we prove it was them?"

"You're pretty good at collecting evidence, Carlita. I'm sure you can figure out a way." Elvira's voice grew muffled. "I hate to sleuth and run, but the gold mining team is heading out soon. They invited me to tag along. Print off what you need and log out of the site."

"Now?"

"Yeah. I want to confirm you logged out."

"Fine." Dernice hit the print screen key. The printer behind her whirred.

Carlita snatched the paper from the tray, confirming it was the page linking the employee identification numbers to Lindsay and Tracy Sterling. "This is good and bad."

"Good, because we're pretty sure we know who was behind the burglaries. Bad because you can't turn it over to the cops," Elvira said. "What you just did could get all of us into a lot of hot water."

"We'll have to figure out a way to use the information to get our own proof."

"Did you log out of the website yet?" Elvira asked.

"Hold your horses. I'm working on it," Dernice muttered. "There. I'm out."

"Thank you." Elvira started to say goodbye.

Her sister stopped her. "Before you go, I want to send you a picture."

"What kinda picture?"

"Hang on." Dernice tracked down a picture of her and Vinnie, one Carlita had just taken, and hit the send button. "Check your messages."

Elvira shrieked. "Vinnie is in town?"

"He is," Carlita said. "He and Brittney showed up last night for a surprise visit."

"Well, this sucks."

"For you," Dernice snorted. "He's a hot babe. Did you notice how cozy we look?"

"Keep your hands off him," Elvira warned.

"Too late." Dernice pumped her fist toward the floor, yanking her arm back. She did it again, mimicking the "lawnmower dance," a viral craze Mercedes and Autumn had recently shown Carlita. "You still have your phone in hand?"

"Of course I do," Elvira snapped. "How do you think I'm talking to you?"

"Touchy touchy." With a look of pure glee, Dernice tapped the top of her phone. "Eat your heart out."

Elvira made a hissing sound. "You had your hands on my man. I've only been gone for a couple of days and you're already hot after my honey."

"I hate to be the bearer of bad news," Carlita said. "Vinnie isn't your honey. He's happily married to Brittney."

"Well, I'm next in line if something happens, and they split up," Elvira said. "I can't believe he let you touch him."

"He put his arm around me. By the way, it was his idea. The arm around me part that is."

"This is so wrong," Elvira grumbled. "How long is he in town?"

"He *and Brittney* are only here for a couple of days." Without thinking, Carlita added, "He's invited us to New Jersey to see his place."

"Sweet," Elvira hooted. "When are we going?"

"*We* aren't going anywhere. You weren't invited." Which wasn't technically the truth. Almost as an afterthought, Vinnie had invited Elvira and the rest of the gang. "I mean, you were sort of invited."

"Did Vinnie invite me or not?" Elvira demanded.

"He did, in a roundabout way, along with Dernice and Luigi. He's going to reserve some rooms for us at the casino's hotel."

"Was this before or after my sister manhandled my man?"

"I didn't manhandle your man. Please note he has his arm around me in the picture."

"Then you must have bribed him," Elvira said. "I'll have to try it next time."

"I thought you had to go," Carlita reminded her.

"I do. I'm walking and talking. In fact, I'm almost there." Elvira started to sound winded. "The air up here is a little dense."

"We don't need you passing out," Carlita said. "Thanks for giving us access to your dark web."

"No problem. Keep me posted. If Sterling's daughters are behind the break-in, I want them to pay for the damages."

"We don't..." Carlita started to say they had no proof. It was too late. Elvira had already disconnected.

"She's all wound up now," Dernice snickered. "I would've loved to have seen the look on her face when she saw the picture of Vinnie and me."

"Me too." Carlita's eyes were drawn to the printout. They had what she considered proof, yet they couldn't use it. Somehow, they would have to figure out a way to link the sisters to the burglaries. "I'm still curious about what the sisters look like."

"Social media. They're young. A hundred bucks says they have profiles."

"You're probably right. Do you mind taking a look?"

"Already on it." Dernice tapped the keys, pulling up a popular social media site. She typed "Lindsay Sterling, Savannah, Georgia" in the search bar. A profile popped up. At the top of the page was a photo of a blonde, a little on the fluffy side with a friendly smile, standing next to another woman with similar features, but thinner.

"Bingo."

"This is Lindsay and Tracy Sterling?"

"Yep."

Carlita adjusted her reading glasses and leaned in, studying their faces. They didn't look like thieves...or burglars. Not that it mattered what they looked like. Looks could be deceiving. Sometimes the most innocent faces masked the evilest intentions. "You said you met them when you were working undercover. What did you think?"

"They were super friendly and the one was very helpful in training me."

Carlita pivoted, curiously eyeing Dernice. "At the risk of not minding my own business, what were they training you to do?"

Her eyes slid to the side. "It's kind of embarrassing."

The way Dernice said it piqued Carlita's interest even more. "An office position?"

"Sort of...kinda."

"Finance?"

"No."

"The service department?"

"Nope."

Carlita snapped her fingers. "I know. A car saleswoman."

"No, although it would have been sweet. I could've made a few extra bucks."

"I give up. I can't think of another office position."

"Okay. Fine. It wasn't an office position. It was car detailing. They had me working out back cleaning vehicles customers traded in."

"It sounds like a dirty job."

"It was. I made Elvira pay me extra for doing her dirty work...literally."

"And the Sterling sisters showed you how to detail the vehicles? I figured they would hold office positions."

"They did. Now that I think about it, I believe Lindsay works in finance."

"Which would be the perfect position to help herself to her father's money. What about Tracy?"

"She was more of a girl Friday, a Jill of all trades," Dernice explained. "As I said, Tracy helped train me."

"And you somehow managed to get office info while working in another department?" Carlita asked.

Dernice tapped the side of her forehead. "I have my ways, which is why Elvira pays me the big bucks."

"Elvira pays you well?"

"It was a joke." Dernice flexed her fingers. "Let's check out Tracy's online profile."

A photo of Tracy Sterling appeared. She wore a black skirted leotard with a fitted tank top. There was no doubt the woman was on the thin side and agile, but was she agile enough to scale the side of a building?

"She looks like she could definitely be a cat burglar. Let's look at the surveillance again." Dernice turned on a second computer monitor and pulled up the recordings from the night of the break-in.

She hit the pause button when burglar one and two appeared. Sliding the computer monitors closer together, the women compared the body sizes, confirming it could have been the Sterling sisters.

"I think we're closing in on the culprits," Carlita finally said. "They tick all the boxes."

"One of them is athletic, while the other is a little larger." Dernice patted her abdomen. "Although there's nothing wrong with fluffy. In fact, I love being fluffy. Food is meant to be enjoyed."

"I couldn't agree more." Carlita drummed her fingers on the desk, her eyes flitting from the still frame to the photo of Tracy Sterling. "How do we prove it's them?"

"We can't roll in there demanding they confess to burglarizing our businesses," Dernice said. "We need concrete proof. If not, Russell Sterling strikes me as the type of man who wouldn't hesitate to sue us for slander."

"Based on his reaction earlier, I believe you may be right."

A commotion near the entrance caught Carlita's attention. As the visitors drew closer, her heart plummeted. "What are they doing here?"

"More good news?" Dernice cleared her throat. "Hopefully, they haven't been monitoring our internet searches."

Chapter 20

Officer Jonkers and Officer Thryce stepped inside the EC Investigative Services' office. "Good day, Ms. Cobb. You remember Officer Thryce."

"I do."

"He and I were contacted by our fraud division. I know our visit is unexpected, but we hoped we could have a minute of your time."

"Of course." Dernice sprang from her chair. She rushed across the room and shook hands with them. "Carlita...Mrs. Taylor and I were just discussing the burglaries, wondering if there were any updates."

"We're still working on it." Jonkers told them they'd received a call via their anonymous tip line. "It was concerning enough that we thought we should bring it to your attention."

Carlita and Dernice exchanged a puzzled look. "A concerning tip came in?"

"The caller insisted one of you, or maybe both of you, are contemplating insurance fraud," Jonkers said.

"Insurance fraud?" Carlita's jaw dropped. "You can't be serious."

"The accusation is very serious." Thryce pinned her with a hard stare. "An insurance fraud conviction means guaranteed prison time and a hefty fine, not to mention civil penalties, along with restitution."

"Because our businesses were burglarized?" Carlita resisted the urge to roll her eyes. "I haven't filed an insurance claim over the vandalism, nor do I intend to."

"Ditto here." Dernice scowled. "This is a ridiculous accusation."

"What about Ken Colby, the other business owner who was burglarized?" Carlita asked. "I can't speak for Ken, but I don't believe he planned to file a claim either, even though he was the one who ended up with the most damage."

"What purpose would someone have to call the hotline and make this sort of claim?" Jonkers asked.

"To try to steer investigators away from the culprits," Carlita said. "From finding out who is behind the vandalism and break-ins."

"Clearly, it was someone who knew about the fundraiser or attended it the other night," Thryce said.

"I agree. I think it was someone who took advantage of the fact most of the area businesses were unattended, giving them the perfect opportunity to break in undetected."

"Even though all of us have burglar alarms and monitored systems," Dernice said.

"You're sure you have no intention of filing an insurance claim?" Jonkers asked.

"Nope. My son, who runs my pawn shop, has already contacted a glass company to come out and repair the damaged window. We haven't addressed the broken drainpipe yet."

"And you?" Thryce motioned to Dernice. "You don't intend to file a claim for the ductwork?"

"I'll admit the idea had crossed my mind. Unfortunately, my sister, the person who owns this building and business, is making me pay the repairs out-of-pocket seeing how I was the one who...damaged it," Dernice said.

The officers excused themselves. They stepped out of the building and onto the sidewalk.

Carlita watched them consult with one another, occasionally looking their way. "I think we're hot on the trail of the Sterling sisters. I'd be curious to find out exactly when the anonymous call came in."

"If it was after you and Pete went over there to question Sterling, it could have been him or his daughters."

The cops stepped back inside. "While we're here, we would like to take another look around upstairs."

"Sure." Dernice motioned for them to follow her to the back of the building and up the stairs.

Carlita gave them a head start before trailing behind. She lingered near the doorway, watching as the pair inspected the vent cover and what was left of the ductwork. "If you don't mind me asking, what time did the anonymous tip about potential insurance fraud come in?"

"Sometime today."

Carlita glanced at her watch. She and Pete had left Sterling Automotive Group's offices a little over two hours ago. If the Sterling sisters were behind the vandalism, break-ins and the automotive company's missing money, there was a good chance Russell Sterling had told Lindsay and Tracy how Pete and Carlita were asking questions. They panicked and placed the anonymous call to throw investigators off and throw their attention on the innocent business owners.

The more she thought about it, the angrier she became. If it was them, the sisters were beginning to look like nothing more than entitled, spoiled brats who had committed a crime—against their own father no less—and had every intention of getting away with it.

If this was the case, and Russell Sterling was covering for them, he wasn't doing his daughters any favors. They needed to be taught a lesson. And if Carlita had her way, she would be the person to help make it happen.

"...is right, Carlita?"

"I...I'm sorry," she apologized. "I wasn't paying attention. What did you say?"

"I said we think these burglaries might be linked to an incident that happened over at Sterling Automotive Group a few weeks ago."

"Yes. We do. In fact, Mr. Sterling, Russell Sterling, was at the fundraiser the other night," Carlita said. "Perhaps you should visit him."

Jonkers frowned. "What makes you think they're linked?"

"The burglaries were similar, except the person or persons who broke into his dealership disarmed his alarm. They never took anything and didn't bother with the safe. As far as I know, no cash was stolen."

Thryce nudged Jonkers. "Have you heard about this case?"

"No, but I intend to look into it."

While the trio talked, Dernice wandered over to the damaged metal and picked at a sharp edge.

"Are you okay?" Carlita asked in a low voice. "You seem a little perturbed."

"I'm still aggravated at myself for getting stuck. I should've known better."

"It can't be too expensive to get the duct replaced."

"I already got a rough estimate over the phone. The guy quoted between a thousand and twelve hundred bucks, subject to change depending on what he found when he got here."

Carlita coughed loudly. "A thousand dollars? Maybe you *should* file a claim."

"No way. I already hinted around to Elvira before the cops showed up on the doorstep after I got the ballpark figure."

"And?"

"She shot it down." Dernice made a double thumbs down. "She seems to think filing a claim will jack up her premium."

"Which would be a legitimate concern. Anytime you file a claim, your rates automatically go up. Personally, I wouldn't go that route unless it was for something catastrophic." Carlita tipped her head to the side, eyeing the opening. "I'm almost positive Tracy Sterling could have easily shimmied through there."

"With a little extra room to boot."

Jonkers, who had been scoping out the overhang and remaining ductwork, made her way over. "Can we borrow your ladder again?"

"Sure. I left it in the other room." Dernice hurried off, returning moments later carrying the ladder.

Thryce ran over and took it from her. Carrying it the rest of the way across the room, he unfolded it and set it near the opening. While the trio looked on, he climbed to the top and peered inside. "You were right."

"About seeing what I believe might be fingerprints?" Jonkers asked.

"Yeah."

The officer pointed to Dernice. "You didn't make it as far as the end of the duct, the section near the point of entry, did you?"

"Nope. Not even close."

"Good. Then hopefully we won't be wasting our time. I'll go grab the fingerprinting kit." She took off, returning within minutes. She set the kit next to the window and lifted the lid.

Carlita crept as close as she dared without getting in the way, watching Jonkers slip on a pair of latex gloves. She prepped the dusting kit and passed the tools to her partner.

Jonkers must've sensed she was being watched and glanced over her shoulder. "I think we're gonna get a good, clean set."

"I hope so. Those burglars made several mistakes."

"Bungling burglars," Jonkers said. "You would be surprised at how bad some crooks are. It's almost as if they want to get caught."

"So you mix the powder, dust the area and then lift the prints?" Carlita asked.

"Correct. Using tape." Jonkers held up a clear piece of glass, the kind used with microscopes. "The tape is placed on these slides, labeled, and then taken down to forensics, where they run it through the database to see if there's a match."

"But if the person who left these prints doesn't have a record, they're useless," Carlita said.

"Basically. Although we hang onto them in the event sometime down the road, there's an arrest and we get a match."

Thryce handed Jonkers the slide. She carefully placed it inside the box. "Whoever it was left a nice set of prints with all four fingers."

Jonkers handed him another slide. Back and forth they went. Clear slide, print slide until they had a copy of all four prints. "I know we've been joking about this, but whoever broke in here was very sloppy."

"Which is good news for us." Dernice crossed her fingers. "Here's to a match and putting these vanburglars behind bars."

"Vanburglars?"

"Vandals plus burglars. Vanburglars."

Jonkers put the tools back inside the box and snapped the lid. "Unfortunately, if we don't get an immediate match, these unsolved cases fall by the wayside."

"I have to admit, it ticks me off to think someone is out there trying to turn victims into potential suspects," Carlita said.

"You would be surprised at how often this happens, typically with the call being placed by the culprits." Thryce folded the ladder and propped it against the wall. "You seem like nice people, honest, hardworking Savannah business owners. We'll do what we can."

"And we appreciate your efforts." Dernice, with Carlita taking the lead, chatted with the officers on their way down the steps and out of the building.

They both thanked her for allowing them to look around again and drove off.

Carlita placed her hands on her hips. "Something tells me the lab won't find a match."

"I would almost bet on it," Dernice said. "If only we could get our hands on prints from Lindsay and Tracy."

She rubbed her chin thoughtfully. "I'm not gonna let this go. We'll come up with a plan to get the prints, one way or another."

Chapter 21

"I'm always down for a Garlucci family hallway potluck." Luigi set a big pot of minestrone, his specialty, on the table in the upper hallway, the designated location of the monthly get-togethers.

Cool Bones, another of Carlita's tenants, arrived a few minutes later, carrying big bowls of barbecue ribs. Tony and Shelby brought baked beans and coleslaw. Autumn Winter wasn't far behind, bringing dessert, a decadent cheesecake. "Sorry this isn't homemade, but it is the best chocolate cheesecake in town."

"Thank you for bringing it." Carlita wheeled a portable cooking station alongside the table. "I'm trying something new. It's tableside smoky pasta burrata. Arnie thought it might be fun to add tableside service at Ravello's. Mercedes and I tried this dish the other day. It was delicious. I offered to give it a trial run and you are gonna be my taste testers."

Cool Bones rubbed his palms together. "Sign me up, anytime."

Pete assembled the ingredients, including spiral pasta cooked perfectly al dente, while the stragglers slowly trickled in.

Dernice showed up with loaves of crusty Italian bread she'd picked up at Colby's Corner Store.

Sam was the last to join them, bringing jugs of sweet and unsweet tea along with cups, plates, plastic ware, and napkins.

"What's all this?" Vinnie gave his mother a quick hug and motioned to the partially prepped pasta dish.

"It's our monthly get-together and the pasta..." Carlita patted the top of the station. "Is part of a tableside service experiment. I'm trying something new."

Pete, who had volunteered to be her sous chef, blended the roasted red peppers, lemon juice, garlic and red pepper flakes before adding chopped walnuts.

While he stood mixing and blending, Carlita cooked the breadcrumbs, lemon zest, smoked paprika and the rest of the red pepper flakes in a saucepan over medium heat. As soon as they were golden brown, she took the pasta, now mixed with the roasted red peppers, and folded in the tomatoes, Parmesan and remaining walnuts.

"I can't wait to dig in." Mercedes licked her lips.

"I hope this is as tasty as the batch Arnie made." Carlita sprinkled the seasoned breadcrumbs over the pasta and topped it with fresh basil.

Tony placed his napkin on his lap. "I feel like we're back in Ma's kitchen up in Queens."

"You know how much I love whipping up an Italian feast." Carlita circled the table, placing generous portions of pasta on each of their plates alongside the other food.

While they feasted, she gazed around, her heart brimming with love for her family and close friends. She only wished Paulie, Gina, and the kids were there. It would have made the dinner complete.

Pete, who was seated to her left, squeezed her hand. "You're thinking about how blessed you are, but still missing the ones who aren't here."

"Including Kris." Pete's only child, his daughter, traveled extensively for her job, which meant visits were few and far between.

Mercedes tapped the table with the end of her fork to get everyone's attention. "Autumn and I want to take the kids to the park tomorrow. We were thinking around ten."

Violet's eyes lit. "The big park with the twisty slides?"

"Yes. The big park."

"I want to go to the park," little Vinnie said.

"We'll swing by Tony and Shelby's place to pick Violet up and then little Vinnie around ten."

Carlita nudged her daughter. "I might have an errand for you tomorrow."

"An errand?"

"The cops stopped by Elvira's earlier and took a set of fingerprints from her ductwork. We need someone to go over to Sterling Automotive Group and try to get prints from Lindsay and Tracy, Sterling's daughters, who work at the business to see if there's a match."

Mercedes grimaced.

"Is there a problem?" her mother asked.

"Sort of. If you remember, Sterling was the flirty guy from the fundraiser the other night. I'm pretty sure he'll recognize me if he sees me again."

"Crud. You're right. I forgot." Carlita rubbed her forehead. "I've been sitting here trying to figure out how to prove Lindsay and Tracy Sterling are behind the burglaries and vandalism."

"You can't just waltz in there and ask them to give you a set," Vinnie said.

"Sterling made a point of telling me his automotive dealership was a family affair. I wonder what the daughters do there." Autumn picked up her cell phone sitting next to her.

"I can save you a search," Dernice said. "Lindsay works in finance. Tracy is kind of the go-to gal. When I was working undercover, she trained me in detailing."

"Why not let the cops handle it?" Tony asked. "I doubt they're gonna come back and try breaking in again."

"Because I'm almost certain they're the ones who called the anonymous tip hotline and accused us of filing a false claim for insurance purposes," Carlita said.

"Seriously?" Sam frowned. "Why?"

"Because Pete and I stopped by to ask Russell Sterling about his break-in. I think he knows his daughters are responsible, and he's covering for them." Carlita laid out her theory about how Russell discovered someone was stealing money from his business and hired EC Investigative Services to figure out who it was. "Dernice went in undercover and tracked down the employee numbers of the individuals associated with the theft."

"Who turned out to be Lindsay and Tracy Sterling," Dernice said. "They somehow found out about the investigation and broke into Elvira's office to get the records before Russell, their father, found out."

"Not knowing it was too late. Elvira had already given him the report with the employee numbers linking them to the theft," Carlita added.

"Ah." Vinnie drummed his fingers on the table. "And now he's trying to cover for them."

"In a nutshell. Whether he knows they're attempting to make us look like insurance fraudsters or not is another story. If we can match the prints found on the ductwork to one of them." Dernice slapped her hands. "Bam! We have our burglars."

"I might have an idea," Autumn said. "Before Russell Sterling began hitting on me the other night, he mentioned my feature programs and seemed interested in having me do a spotlight about him and his family business. In fact, he was practically begging me."

Carlita's scalp tingled. "Autumn, you might be our in."

"There is something else…" Her voice trailed off.

"What is it?"

"I don't mind setting something up, but I might need to bring Luigi along as my bodyguard to keep him in line."

"I wouldn't trust him," Mercedes said.

"I never got that impression, although Pete was with me when we met with him, not to mention you're both younger and prettier than an old woman like me."

"I think you're a gorgeous woman," her husband said.

Carlita squeezed his arm. "I love you, Pete Taylor, but you know what I mean."

"Do you think you can arrange something fairly quickly?" Dernice asked. "The sooner the better, before his two conniving daughters dream up some other way to throw us under the bus."

Autumn shoved her chair back. "Let me make a couple of quick phone calls. I'll be right back."

"If you don't mind, I would like to listen in."

"Not at all." Autumn waited for Carlita to step inside her apartment and closed the door behind them. She tracked down her boss at the station first, asking if she could squeeze in a local business interview the following day.

"The only possible time would be around noon tomorrow. It would be tight."

"Tight but not impossible."

"I dunno." For a minute, Carlita was certain he was going to say no, but Autumn was very persuasive at convincing him that viewers would be interested in the family-run business.

Finally, he relented. "But only if you can get Wes, your camera guy, to agree."

"Would you mind transferring me over to him?"

"I suppose. If you weren't one of our most requested reporters, I would've said no," her boss grumbled.

"I have the highest viewership in the area."

"Which is why I'm reluctantly saying yes."

"Thanks, boss."

"You're welcome."

With a few transfers, Autumn reached Wes, who didn't seem to mind. "Did you run it by the department's head honcho?"

"He told me as long as you were okay with it, we could go."

"You said Sterling Automotive Group? What location?"

"The location?"

Carlita whispered the address and Autumn repeated it out loud. "If Sterling can't do it, I guess we'll have to try for another day."

As soon as Autumn ended the call, she dialed Sterling Automotive Group's main number and put the call on speaker, allowing Carlita to listen in. Using her professional reporter voice, she asked to speak with Russell Sterling. "He and I chatted at a fundraiser the other night. I have a time slot for an upcoming airing on our station and wondered if he might be interested."

"What did you say your name was?"

"Autumn Winter. I'm a reporter with Channel Eleven News."

"Please hold."

Elevator music ensued.

It abruptly ended. "Russell Sterling speaking."

"Hello, Mr. Sterling. This is Autumn Winter. I'm not sure if you remember me. We met at a fundraiser a couple of nights ago. It was for my brother who owns the Shades of Ink tattoo shop."

"I remember you. You're the petite lady who was rocking a red dress."

"I was wearing a red dress."

"We spoke about your job at the station and how you were able to get some publicity for the fundraiser, which is how I found out about it."

"Correct. You mentioned being interested in a feature story as well."

"Yes. Absolutely."

"As luck would have it, I have an opening tomorrow at noon. It's a half an hour time slot. Would you be available to do a brief segment?"

"Of course," Sterling said. "I'll make time. You mentioned noon?"

"Correct," Autumn confirmed.

"Come to the front desk and ask for me." He gave her the address.

"We will."

Sterling thanked her and started to end the call.

Carlita mouthed the words, "daughters."

"Wait. Before you go, you mentioned it being a family business. The station managers are interested in this angle."

"I have a few family members working for Sterling Automotive Group, including my two daughters."

"Do you think it would be possible for them to be on hand for a brief cameo?"

"Definitely. Their names are Lindsay and Tracy Sterling."

"Perfect. I'll see you tomorrow at noon." Autumn ended the call and lifted her hand.

Carlita slapped it, giving her a high five. "Thank you, Autumn. This is nothing short of a miracle."

The women returned to the table.

"Well?" Mercedes asked. "Any luck?"

"We're on for a noon interview tomorrow with Sterling *and* his daughters," Autumn said. "My only problem now is figuring out how to get Lindsay's and Tracy's fingerprints."

"It could be tricky," Carlita said. "Sterling is already suspicious."

While they mulled over how they could pull off keeping Sterling distracted while obtaining a set of prints from his daughters, Carlita noticed Brittney nudge her husband and whisper in his ear.

"Hey, Ma. Brittney has an idea."

"I'm open to any and all suggestions," Carlita said.

"I could be a distraction."

Brittney, a beautiful woman, a willowy blonde with a Marilyn Monroe air about her. She turned heads wherever she went. In fact, more than once, Vinnie had joked about having to keep an eye on the men who ogled her.

"You could definitely distract Sterling. Maybe a little too much," Carlita said.

"Brittney is as tough as nails. Sterling will draw back a nub if he tries to get too friendly," Vinnie said.

It was true. Although drop-dead gorgeous, Brittney also possessed a hard edge, courtesy of being raised by Vito Castellini, who had been the head of the mob family for decades. She had even witnessed her attacking a woman after being provoked. Something told Carlita she wouldn't hesitate to defend herself again, if necessary.

"Are you sure you wanna do it?"

"I want to help," Brittney said.

Luigi dropped his napkin on the table and lifted his hand. "Speaking from experience and being around the Castellini family for many years, I can assure you Brittney Castellini Garlucci will hold her own."

"Okay, but just know this whole thing could blow up in our faces," Carlita warned.

"We won't know until we try," Autumn said.

"What time did you plan to go over there?" Pete asked.

"Noon."

"Perfect. I have a special family and friends event planned for tomorrow afternoon. Everyone needs to meet out in front of Ravello's at three on the dot." Pete did a quick count of heads. "I know it's short notice, but I'm hoping everyone here can make it. I will need a head count."

"I got a gig over at the convention center," Luigi said. "Will we be done by eight?"

"Yes," Pete said. "I have our special...event planned from three until seven. Jeans, shorts, any sort of casual attire will be fine. Make sure you wear sturdy walking shoes. We will be doing some walking and taking stairs."

"What about the kids?" Shelby patted Violet's arm.

"Kids, adults. Young and old."

"Bummer. Unfortunately, I have to work," Autumn said. "But...I get out at five. Maybe I can make it for the second half of the festivities."

"I know you can." Pete, with a mischievous twinkle in his eye, pulled Autumn aside and began whispering in her ear. She nodded a few times. "Where's the schedule?"

"I'll send you a copy so you'll know where to catch up with us."

"Thanks, Pete."

Carlita waited for her husband to return to his seat and kissed his cheek. "You're so thoughtful. I'm sure we'll have a blast."

"Either a bomb or a blast," he joked. "Something tells me with this crowd, it will be the latter."

While the others began passing around the dessert, an uneasiness settled over Carlita. Sterling. His conniving daughters. Autumn and now Brittney. What could possibly go wrong?

Everything. Everything could go wrong. Hopefully, it wouldn't.

Chapter 22

Autumn, Brittney and her camera guy, Wes, gathered next to the Channel Eleven News van.

The plan is to interview Mr. Sterling, kind of get a side story about how the daughters came to work with their father."

"How are you gonna get a set of fingerprints?" Brittney asked.

"Hopefully, with this." Autumn patted her back pocket. "My cell phone, for some still shots. I'll offer to take a few selfies."

"Or with mine," Wes said. "If we can remember to keep our fingers off the glass we should be good to go."

"I might have an idea or two, as well." Brittney said. "You're a great guy for offering to help Autumn. She's lucky to have you on her team."

Wes blushed, his cheeks turning a tinge of pink at Brittney's compliment. "Autumn has had her share of exciting escapades with the Garlucci family."

"Did she fill you in on what's going on?"

"Yeah. Sterling is a pretty big name around these parts. I met his daughters a few years ago at a party," Wes said. "They were a trip."

"A trip in a good way or a bad way?" Brittney asked.

"They have a level of entitlement," he said. "We were at a New Year's Eve party downtown. The sisters ended up getting picked up for disorderly conduct."

"So they have police records?" Autumn's brows knitted. "I wonder why the investigators haven't been able to match their fingerprints to the ones found on Elvira's ductwork."

"*If* it was them," Brittney said. "Maybe it wasn't them and we're after the wrong people."

"Carlita seems certain. There are too many clues pointing to it being Lindsay and Tracy," Autumn said.

Wes made a timeout with his hands. "I didn't finish. Russell Sterling ran right down there while they were putting the cuffs on the troublemakers. He pulled a few strings and got his daughters released."

"Before they were booked?"

"Yep. Some others who were part of the group weren't so lucky."

"Daddy to the rescue," Autumn quipped. "Going back to the entitlement angle."

"They sound like brats," Brittney said.

"You'll see what I mean."

"Do you think they'll remember you?" Autumn asked.

"Maybe. There were a lot of people around that night." Wes, who had been fiddling with his gear, made an unhappy sound.

"What's wrong?" Autumn asked. "Trouble with the audio equipment again?"

"Yeah. It's on the fritz. I thought it was fixed, but testing it just now, it cut out."

"Crud." Autumn cast a wary gaze toward the front door. "If we don't do this today, we might not have time to come back."

"Let's get 'er done and keep our fingers crossed that it doesn't go out." Gathering up the gear, the trio strolled inside the dealership at exactly eleven fifty-nine. As soon as the receptionist found out who they were, she whisked them down the hall to a conference room in the back.

While they waited for Sterling and his daughters, Brittney stood off to the side, quietly watching them set up the equipment.

The door flew open. Russell Sterling appeared. "Hello, Ms. Winter."

"Hello, Mr. Sterling." Autumn forced a smile and extended her hand. "It's nice to see you again," she fibbed.

"Same here."

Autumn motioned to Wes. "This is my cameraman, Wes."

Sterling shook his hand, but his eyes were on Brittney. "And who is this gorgeous creature?"

"My...apprentice, Brittney," Autumn said. "She...uh...is learning all about live journalism."

"And what a stunning reporter she will be." He grasped Brittney's hand. Instead of shaking it, he kissed the top, lingering a little too long for her liking.

She jerked it away and wiped it on her slacks.

Sterling either didn't notice or didn't care. "Shall we get started? I thought we could record a small segment in here and then move onto my office."

Autumn craned her neck. "Where are your daughters?"

"Unfortunately, I don't think they'll be able to make it. Lindsay is with a customer. Tracy is running an errand."

Autumn's heart plummeted. "I was hoping to cover the family angle, how wonderful of an opportunity it was for your daughters—women—to break into what most consider a profession dominated by men."

"Lindsay will try very hard to wrap things up. She's interested in the idea of expanding her horizons and embarking on a career with a more public following," Sterling said. "She's a natural. So is Tracy."

"Then I hope both of them can make it." Autumn picked up her microphone. "We'll start with me asking you a little about the history of your company. Maybe you could throw out a few facts and figures, how many people you employ, interesting information along those lines."

Sterling straightened his tie. "I'm ready."

Autumn counted from three down to one. Wes signaled the camera was rolling. She flawlessly started her spiel, explaining to viewers where she was and what the segment was about. "I'm here with Russell Sterling. Many of you might already know Mr. Sterling, who is a prominent local businessman in the automotive sales and service industry."

She asked him how he got started. He spouted off some numbers and even shared a funny little anecdote about a raccoon who broke into a car and how they called animal services to rescue him.

A flitting movement caught Autumn's eye. A woman, about her age and slightly overweight, slipped into the room. She ended the segment and signaled for Wes to stop the recording. "Hello."

"Hello. I hope I'm not interrupting."

"Not at all, dear." Sterling crossed the room. He placed a light hand on her back. "Autumn, Brittney, Wes, this is my daughter, Lindsay."

Autumn shook hands with her. "It's nice to meet you. Thank you for joining us."

"Sorry if I'm late. I was with a customer and got here as fast as I could."

"Your timing is perfect." Autumn explained she'd finished the first segment and suggested they move to Sterling's office for part two of the interview.

"Excellent."

Exiting the conference room, they walked along the long hall to the office at the end. On the wall and in big, bold gold letters was Russell Sterling's name.

Autumn hesitated in the doorway, noting the scent of expensive leather, along with the faint aroma of cigar smoke mingled with something else. A pup with a shaggy coat and big floppy ears scrambled off a doggie bed and trotted over.

"This is Chevy," Lindsay said.

"Hi, Chevy." Autumn scratched his ears and patted his back.

Wes greeted him.

Brittney hovered near the wall, nervously licking her lips.

"He won't bite," Lindsay said.

"Chevy looks friendly. Unfortunately, I'm allergic to dogs." Brittney cautiously stepped back.

"I'll put him in the courtyard." Lindsay led him to a set of sliders and let the pup out.

Sterling rubbed his palms together. "Where would you like to start?"

Autumn surveyed the layout of the room, her mind racing. She needed to get a set of Lindsay's prints, but how? "Why don't you sit behind the desk? Your daughter can take a chair across from you, maybe look like you're going over some papers for the first shot."

Brittney tottered across the room and began fumbling around in her purse. "I noticed your hair is a little mussed up, Lindsay." She reached into her designer bag, pulled out a folding compact, and handed it to her. "You can borrow my mirror."

"Thanks." The woman took the compact. She flipped it open and began studying her reflection, turning her head from right to left. "I don't see what you're talking about."

"Over on this side." Brittney pointed to a section of hair that was out of view. "Maybe if you tilt the mirror a little more to the side. You might want to hold it tighter. My compact is slippery."

Lindsay tightened her grip, shifting the mirror and reflecting it downward. "I still don't see it."

Brittney reached out and hesitated. "May I?"

"Sure."

She smoothed the woman's hair. "Perfect."

"Thank you." Lindsay held out the mirror.

Brittney carefully snapped it shut and placed it back inside her purse. Autumn turned her head. She caught Brittney's eye and her "protégé" winked.

Wes began positioning Sterling and his daughter, directing them in order to get the best angle for the camera shot.

Meanwhile, Autumn crept across the room and joined Brittney. "That was genius," she said in a low voice.

"Thanks." Brittney beamed. "One down, one to go. I might have another trick up my sleeve."

"We're ready," Wes announced.

"Let's get to it." Autumn segued into her second segment, asking all the right questions, wrapping up the final portion of the interview seamlessly. Unfortunately, there was still no sign of Sterling's other daughter. "Is Tracy going to make it?"

"I'll send her a text." Lindsay pulled her phone from her pocket and tapped the screen. "She's running behind. How much longer will you be here?"

Autumn glanced at her watch. She and Wes needed to head to their next taping. "Only a few more minutes."

"Bummer," Lindsay said. "Tracy is bummed."

"So are we," Brittney said.

The trio reluctantly packed up their gear and exited the building, trudging toward their van which was parked next to Carlita's car that Brittney had borrowed.

Autumn set her backpack on the floor and heaved a heavy sigh. "Well, mission half accomplished."

"Hopefully, it's the half that gives us a match," Brittney said.

"With the way my luck runs, I'm gonna guess we fingerprinted the wrong sister." Autumn nudged

Brittney's arm. "But you pulled off a master move. You did a great job of collecting potential evidence."

"Carlita's tricks of the sleuthing trade must have rubbed off on me. It was kinda fun. Thanks for letting me tag along."

"I'm glad you enjoyed it." Autumn slid the van's side door shut. "Because based on what we find, we might be returning for round two."

Chapter 23

"I have some good news and some bad news," Autumn said.

Carlita braced herself. "I'll take the good news first."

"We met with Russell Sterling. I can almost guarantee he didn't suspect a thing."

"Wonderful. Were you able to get a set of fingerprints from his daughters?"

"That's where the bad news comes in. We were only able to get them from one. Actually." Autumn motioned to Brittney. "Brittney was clever in tricking Lindsay into giving us a set."

"By loaning her my compact."

"Good girl." Carlita beamed proudly. "I'm sure Sterling thought he was in heaven. Two beautiful women in the same room."

"He definitely has a roving eye." Brittney reached into her purse and removed the compact Lindsay had borrowed. "I've been careful not to touch this. Hopefully, you'll be able to get a good set of prints."

"I'll call Officer Jonkers and tell her we think we might have the fingerprints of a potential suspect," Carlita said.

"The only downside is if it's not a match and we have to get Tracy's prints, investigators might not be interested, thinking we're wasting their time."

"It does present a dilemma. I wonder if Dernice can help." Carlita made a quick call to the woman, telling her they had a set of Lindsay's prints and explaining the situation.

"You're right. The cops aren't gonna want to feel like they're chasing their tails. Elvira has a friend who works down at the precinct."

The call ended after Dernice promised to see what she could do.

"I hate to sleuth and run, but I gotta head back to work. I'll catch up with you later for the f-." Autumn caught herself and abruptly stopped. "For the fun times after I get out of work."

"Thank you for your help," Carlita said. "With any luck, we'll soon find out if Lindsay's prints match."

"If not, I told Autumn I wouldn't mind helping again," Brittney said.

Tink. Carlita's cell phone chimed. It was Dernice, asking her to bring the compact over ASAP. "It looks like we might find out if we have a match sooner rather than later."

Carlita parted ways with the women in the alley outside of Ravello's. Dernice must've been waiting for her because she hadn't even made it to her back door when it flew open and she appeared. "I finagled a time slot in the forensic department's lab. A woman who works there is a friend of

Elvira's. She promised to get right on examining the prints if I could bring them to her in the next few minutes. Where are they?"

Carlita held up a clear plastic bag. "Lindsay Sterling's prints are on this compact. If they can match them to the ones taken from the ductwork, we have our burglar, or at least one of them."

"And if not?"

"Autumn and Brittney offered to try again, to track down Tracy."

"If you ask me, we have less of a chance in getting a match," Dernice said. "Tracy was the more athletic of the two."

"Based on how many roadblocks we've encountered, I would have to agree." Carlita handed her the bag and thanked her.

"See you at three." Dernice scurried down the alley. She hopped into her work van and hit the gas, throwing gravel as the vehicle careened around the corner.

Carlita watched her speed off. "Something tells me she's gonna make it there at warp speed, no problem."

*****

With time left before Pete's surprise outing, Carlita stopped by the pawn shop to cover for Tony so he could run home. She went over the books, thrilled to discover business was picking back up.

Although fall was still considered the pawn shop's "off season," the holidays were within sight, which meant the fourth quarter would help their bottom line immensely.

Not only was Ravello's already getting holiday bookings but her food truck was also scheduled for a wide range of holiday events throughout December.

All in all, the Garlucci family businesses were doing well. According to Pete, his pirate ship and restaurant were also humming right along.

Tony returned from his break and Carlita headed back to the apartment. Brittney, Vinnie, and her grandson were gone. She found a handwritten note letting them know they had taken little Vinnie to the nearby wildlife center, but promised they would be back in time for Pete's surprise.

Carlita tidied the kitchen and took Rambo for a walk. She and the pup meandered along the river, turning around when they reached the end of River Street.

Halfway back, Pete phoned, asking where she was. "How did Autumn and Brittney's fact-finding mission go?"

"It was semi-successful." Carlita told him what had happened. "Dernice knows someone who works at the police station. She's going to see if there's a match between Lindsay Sterling's fingerprints and those found on Elvira's ductwork. I have a feeling they aren't going to."

"Because you think it was Sterling's other daughter?"

"Yep. However, we won't know unless we try. Maybe we'll be pleasantly surprised."

"And then what? You contact Jonkers and Thryce to let them know?" Pete asked.

"That's the plan."

"The reason I'm calling is Arvid Poindexter and Janet Gigowski want to meet with me. They have their final report about the excavation downstairs."

"And they want to let you know what they found?"

"Correct."

"Elvira is going to be bummed."

"Maybe they did it on purpose," Pete joked.

"Waited until they knew she was out of town to turn over the results?" Carlita laughed out loud. "It's possible."

"Anyway, they should be here any minute."

"I'm about a block away." Carlita told Pete she would drop Rambo off at home and catch up with him.

Picking up the pace, she fast-tracked it to the apartment before making a beeline for the stairway leading to the tunnel system. Pete stood near the top watching for her.

"Are they here?"

"I see them now." Pete flagged them down and waited for the pair to catch up.

"Good to see you again, Pete and Carlita." Arvid shook hands. "Thank you for agreeing to meet with us on such short notice."

"You're welcome. It sounded important."

"I know there has been some concern over how long this project has been taking. Janet...Ms. Gigowski and I received the final results from the archaeological team this morning and thought we would wrap this up expeditiously, considering how patient you've been."

"Is Elvira Cobb joining us?" Gigowski asked.

"It's your lucky day," Carlita said. "She's in Alaska."

"Alaska?" Arvid pressed on the bridge of his glasses. "I believe she mentioned she was traveling there. Would you rather we wait to go over the findings when she returns?"

"No," Carlita and Pete said in unison.

"To be honest, I think it might be better if she isn't here, depending on the results."

"Because you're not sure how she'll react," Gigowski said.

"Oh, we know how she'll react," Pete said. "If you found something, she's going to want to tear the place apart. If you haven't found anything, she'll have a full-blown meltdown."

"And then she'll want to tear the excavation site apart," Carlita joked.

"We can go over the results in your office, but it would probably be best if we discuss a few specific findings at the site."

"Shall we?" Pete descended the steps. Arvid and Janet followed behind, with Carlita bringing up the rear.

It had been a couple of weeks since the last time she'd visited the dig site, mainly because she didn't want to bother the workers. The other reason was because there were so many people it was a tight fit, and being down there made her feel slightly claustrophobic.

Elvira, on the other hand, had swung by every day to check on the progress. Carlita secretly suspected it was because she wanted to keep their feet to the fire and the project moving forward.

After unlocking each of the doors and another series of locks securing the property, Pete and the others finally reached the large opening, the entrance to the excavation site. He flipped a switch and turned the floodlights on.

The tools and equipment the team had brought in were gone. The ground, only days earlier littered with piles of dirt, was smooth and flat. It reminded Carlita of what it had looked like the day they had blown a hole in the wall and gotten their first glimpse of the inside.

Pete let out a low whistle. "The equipment has been cleaned up and shipped out."

"Part of our agreement was to leave the site in the same condition we found it," Arvid said. "I hope it meets your approval."

"More than meets it."

He held up a set of keys. "Thank you for giving our team a set of keys. Feel free to change the locks. I can assure you the group assigned to this dig were professionals. I doubt they made copies, but then again..."

"I may change them if only for the fact I suspect Elvira made a set for herself," Pete said. "I'm dying to know—what's the verdict?"

Taking turns, Arvid and Janet went into a long, detailed explanation about the techniques used to test the soil and artifacts they found during the excavation.

From what Pete had told Carlita, the team had found period pieces...pottery, some tools and even a few small gems, similar to the ones the couple had found the first day.

"The testing confirms our theory. The pieces, coins and gems date back to around 1730."

"Which is when the Parrot House Restaurant was built." Pete scratched the stubble on his chin. "I'm not surprised, considering my family history and what I know about my ancestors."

"Who were a rowdy bunch of plundering marauders," Janet said. "And I don't mean to speak ill of your ancestors."

"You described them perfectly. They were a colorful bunch, known to have some...shall we say...questionable behavior?"

"Including kidnapping drunk men, smuggling them on board pirate ships and using them for free labor after they set sail? Thank goodness Pete hasn't carried on his ancestors' traditions." Carlita sucked in a breath. "So, what's the final result? Is what you found going to put Pete's place on the map?"

Chapter 24

"I would love to tell you the answer is yes," Arvid said. "Unfortunately, despite our extensive excavation and precise examination of what was found, we believe and have confirmed there is nothing else—no buried treasure, no buckets of doubloons to make you rich and famous."

"Which is a roundabout way of telling us there's nothing here," Carlita bluntly replied.

"In a nutshell."

"Having kicked around the site while your team was searching, I have to admit I'm not surprised," Pete said. "Elvira won't be happy."

"To put it mildly," Carlita said.

Arvid handed Pete a brown envelope. "I'm sorry. It wasn't what we had hoped. Janet and I would like to thank you for your hospitality, for allowing us the opportunity to search the site and working with us to reach this disappointing conclusion."

Pete glanced at the contents. "I have a question. Although there weren't any significant findings, we noticed drag marks when we first blew the wall out, meaning at some point there was a smaller vessel right here, in this exact spot."

"Without a doubt," Janet nodded.

Pete shifted his gaze. "There could be more items, artifacts, pieces of history beyond these walls waiting to be recovered."

"It's possible," Arvid agreed. "Would you like us to do some preliminary groundwork and determine the next step in excavating additional property?"

Carlita was tempted to add her two cents but kept quiet. It needed to be Pete's decision...one she hoped he would realize wasn't in their best interest, mainly because it would mean tearing up the restaurant's parking lot, the courtyard, basically all the outdoor space for who knew how long.

It would be disruptive to his business, to his customers, and to them. Yet, it was a choice he might regret down the road. And Carlita didn't want to be the one to talk him out of it if he wanted to continue searching.

She knew what Elvira would say. In fact, if Elvira was there, she would have already asked the question. Carlita was glad she wasn't.

He cast his wife a questioning look.

"It's up to you, Pete." She rattled off the negatives. "On the flip side, you might always wonder if there was something on the property, some long-lost treasure or family history waiting to be discovered."

"The decision is yours," Arvid said. "Would our team be on board to keep going? The answer is a resounding yes. Don't get me wrong, they're still thrilled about what they have found. But Carlita is right. It would be a major undertaking. We would have to restrict access to this entire property, affecting your business and livelihood."

Pete rubbed the back of his neck. "I'll give it some thought," he finally said. "For now, I thank you and your team for all the hard work. If I decide to pursue that avenue, I'll let you know."

Carlita hung around while her husband escorted Arvid and Janet upstairs. He joined her a short time later, a thoughtful expression on his face. She could tell he was torn. "It's a big decision."

"I'm thinking about how long it took them to work in this small area." Pete shoved his hands in his pockets and spun in a slow circle. "Imagine the time, not to mention the level of disruption involved in excavating an area the size of our parking lot."

"And beyond."

Pete tapped the top of the envelope. "I say we hold off on telling anyone what we found out until after

Elvira returns and we can give her the results in person."

Carlita made a zipping motion across her lips. "My lips are sealed."

He knelt on the ground, scooped up a handful of loose dirt and sifted it through his fingers. "It's a relief to have it over. I suppose I should change the locks before Elvira gets home."

"Because we both know she won't accept the results and will want to do some digging herself."

Pete slowly stood. "At least we have a few days of a reprieve. The calm before the storm."

"Before the storm returns to Savannah." Carlita slipped her arm through his. "I've been wondering, are you going to give me a hint about our special outing?"

"No. All you need to know is to dress comfortably, wear good walking shoes and maybe bring a jacket in case it gets chilly."

"Will we be outdoors?"

Pete mulled over her question. "Yes, and no. Both indoors and outdoors."

"Will it be something where I'll want to take pictures?"

"Absolutely. It's not often we get most of the family in the same place at the same time. In fact, I volunteer to be the official photographer."

Carlita playfully punched him in the arm. "You're not giving me good clues."

"That inquisitive mind of yours never rests." Pete kissed the top of her head. "It's getting late. Time to get ready to head over to the meeting spot so you can find out what your surprise is."

It didn't take Carlita long to slip into a pair of comfortable stretch pants, a festive fall top, and casual walking shoes. Pete had a minor emergency he needed to handle downstairs in the restaurant and took off, promising he wouldn't be long.

After he left, Carlita thought about the compact with Lindsay's fingerprints and wondered how Dernice's contact was doing on verifying a match. Hopefully, she would have good news when she caught up with them for the outing.

While she waited, she pulled up the surveillance videos from the pawn shop's break-in. Carlita zoomed in on the person scaling the wall. They disappeared before reappearing, nimbly balancing both feet on the brick exterior. All the while, they kept a tight grip on the rope and drainpipe, traveling down until they lost their grip and fell the rest of the way.

She hit the pause button when their accomplice, also clad in dark clothes, approached the side of the building.

Carlita hit the play button again. The bulkier of the two shoved the rope into their backpack. Although the burglar who fell had a noticeable limp, they moved at a quick clip, disappearing into the dark night, heading toward Elvira's place.

"Sorry it took so long." Pete strode down the hall and stepped in behind his wife.

Carlita's pulse ticked up a notch when he got closer, breathing in his cologne—her favorite—a woodsy masculine scent with a hint of citrus. "You smell nice," she murmured.

"Thank you." He nuzzled her neck. "You smell nice too."

"I spritzed on your favorite perfume." Carlita shifted, wrapping her arms around him. Their eyes met. "I love you, Pete Taylor, more than you'll ever know."

"I love you, Carlita." He lifted her hand and kissed the top. "You compliment me in every way. You don't know how many times I've thanked God he convinced you to give a salty old pirate a chance."

"And you gave a mobster's wife a chance, even after finding out about the skeletons in my closet, knowing more could pop up at any time."

"It keeps our life interesting, doesn't it?" Pete teased. "The pirate's life for a former mobster's wife."

"Exciting in spades." Carlita turned the computer off and reached for her jacket. "We had better get going. It's almost three."

"Almost time for an exciting afternoon with the whole gang...and maybe more."

"Maybe more what?"

Pete pressed a finger to his wife's lips. "If I told you now, it would ruin the surprise."

On the way out, Carlita turned the table lamp on. Because it was such a nice day and they didn't have far to go, the couple walked the short distance to Ravello's. During the stroll, they talked about the fundraiser and how thrilled they were for Steve and Paisley.

At the intersection, Pete and Carlita crossed the street, passing by Annie Dowton's real estate office. After checking for traffic, they crossed again.

Up ahead, Carlita could see her sons and their families, along with Mercedes, Sam, Luigi, and Dernice, standing there.

As they drew closer, she noticed several others. She abruptly stopped in her tracks. "Is that who I think it is?"

"Yep," Pete beamed. "Believe it or not, I almost didn't pull this off."

Chapter 25

"They're here." Carlita ran toward her youngest son, Paulie, who stood talking to his brothers. His triplets and wife, Gina, who held baby Melody, were by his side.

"Paulie, Gina." Carlita hugged them both, her throat clogging. "You're here."

"Better late than never, Ma," Paulie kidded.

Pete, a mischievous twinkle in his eye, caught up with his wife. He shook Paulie's hand. "We almost got busted a few minutes ago over at the house."

Carlita pressed her hand to her chest. "You were at our place?"

"Remember the minor emergency I had to take care of? It was these guys. Paulie didn't know I planned to surprise you, so they came over."

Mercedes picked up. "Pete called me and asked if Paulie and the gang could hang out for a few minutes."

"While we were waiting, we got to meet this beautiful little girl." Gina cuddled Melody close while placing her free arm around Violet. "Gracie, Noel and PJ couldn't wait to see their cousin Violet."

"They brought me a present, Nana." Violet showed her a new watercolor set. "It's from New York."

The group all began talking at once—Tony, Vinnie, Paulie, Mercedes, their families, the kids. It was one big, joyful reunion. Finally, Dernice caught Carlita's eye and motioned her off to the side.

"Thanks again for inviting Luigi and me to the family fun."

"I'm glad you could make it. I'm sure whatever Pete has planned will be great." Carlita rubbed her palms together. "As far as I'm concerned, we could hang out, do nothing, and it would be the perfect way to end the day."

"It might not be all sunshine and lollipops."

Carlita sobered. "Uh-oh. You have bad news?"

"Lindsay Sterling's prints didn't match the ones on the ductwork."

"I was afraid of that. I took another look at the surveillance footage a little while ago. If Tracy is the thinner of the two, she was the burglar who climbed the pawn shop wall and busted the window."

"And broke into Elvira's place. So, it looks like we need to figure out how to get Tracy's fingerprints."

Brittney crept closer, catching the tail end of their conversation. "I'm guessing from the looks on your faces that the prints didn't match."

"Nope."

"We can try to get a set tomorrow," Brittney said. "Autumn offered to go back to Sterling's office."

Carlita felt a tap on her shoulder. She turned to find Mercedes standing behind her. "Hey, Ma. Are you talking about the burglaries?"

"Yeah. Lindsay's fingerprints didn't match the ones found on Elvira's ductwork."

"Bummer."

"So, we might have to take Autumn up on her offer to go back to Sterling's place."

"And me. I would love to go with her," Brittney said. "It was fun."

Beep. Beep. Reese and her trolley rounded the corner. Instead of pulling up at the designated stop, she eased alongside the curb where the group had gathered.

Pete gave her a friendly wave and pivoted. "Hey, guys and gals!"

"Shhh." Violet held a finger to her lips. "Grandpa Pete wants to tell us something."

"Thank you, Violet, and thank you everyone for joining Carlita and me for what we hope will be a fun family outing. Most, if not all, of you already know Reese, our designated driver."

Reese clambered down the steps and joined Pete. She gave the group a mock salute. "Welcome Garlucci gang."

Pete continued. "When I found out Vinnie and his family, along with Paulie and his tribe, were coming down to visit, I enlisted Reese's help." He reached into his jacket pocket and removed a small stack of paper cards. "This afternoon is all about relaxing, cruising around downtown Savannah and enjoying some good food."

A spontaneous round of applause ensued. Pete waited until it quieted down. "Not Ravello's or the Parrot House's delicious cuisine, but other excellent cuisine. Savannah is home to some of the country's finest restaurants, many of which Carlita and I never have time to visit because wc're always so busy."

"In other words, you're all taking a chartered food tour. You'll be the only group getting on and the only group getting off at each of the restaurants." Reese reached into her side window, removed a "Private Party. Not in Service," posterboard sign from inside and stuck it in the display window.

"Without further ado, climb aboard." Pete stood near the steps, handing out the schedule of stops. Carlita took her copy and studied the list. It was filled with popular downtown eateries, many boasting five-star ratings. "We're going to each of these places?"

"We are. It's all arranged," Pete said. "I've reserved times at each location with a set menu. Some with appetizers, some with entrees, others with drinks and a couple with desserts."

"This must have cost a small fortune." Carlita's head shot up. "The Olde Blue House? We'll have a two-hour wait to get a table."

"Not us. We have reservations. You'll see."

The more Carlita read, the more excited she became. All were top-notch restaurants. As she perused the list, she quickly discovered Pete had knocked it out of the park.

"You even reserved a spot at the Tapas Room, the old movie theater?"

"I did." Pete patted his pocket. "Remember the other night when we were watching Autumn's food show, and you said the menu sounded interesting?" He didn't wait for her to reply. "This is your chance to check it out."

"Leopold's. You have Leopold's Ice Cream on here."

"Which will be our last stop. For the kids. You know how much Violet loves their double chocolate chip ice cream."

Carlita shifted her gaze, glimpsing Violet, who was sandwiched in between Gracie and Noel. The children were smiling and chattering back and forth.

"Pete Taylor." She hugged him. "You stinker. You got all my kids here, booked a trolley with Reese and are treating us to a night out. I can't even begin to guess how you pulled this off without me having a clue."

"It was tricky, I must admit."

"I bet."

"Isn't this what Savannah is all about? Good food, good friends, and family." Pete lowered his voice. "Seeing the look on your face when you spotted Paulie and his family was worth all the effort."

Carlita could feel her lower lip tremble. She had loved her husband Vinnie with all her heart, had been a faithful wife, raised wonderful children and been his staunchest supporter, but Vinnie would never have planned something like this for her. It never would have even crossed his mind.

"I don't know what to say." She clasped his hand, her heart full, when she noticed all three of her sons talking and laughing. The wives sat chatting, smiling, catching up.

"Seeing you happy is all I want," Pete said in a low voice.

"All aboard!!" Reese waved her hand to get Pete's and Carlita's attention. "Are you two gonna stand there all night and make googly eyes at each other or are we gonna hit all the hip, hot and happening restaurants in Savannah?"

Pete smiled, the corner of his eyes crinkling. "Reese is right. The clock is ticking. Shall we?"

"You bet. Let's get this show on the road." Carlita boarded the trolley, stepping into an atmosphere of warmth and love only family and close friends could provide. *This* was what it meant to be a part of the Garlucci-Taylor family.

It would be a night to remember. Of that, Carlita had no doubt.

Chapter 26

Carlita snuggled closer to Pete, feeling the rumble of the trolley as it clickety-clacked along the brick street. It was a beautiful afternoon. The perfect kind of day to don her tourist hat and see the sights through the eyes of her children and grandchildren.

Luigi and Dernice sat cozied up a few seats back. Tony and Shelby sat across from each other with their small family. Vinnie and Brittney were on one bench seat with baby Vinnie sandwiched between them. Sam sat with his arm casually draped across Mercedes' shoulders. He whispered in her ear and she giggled.

Reese was in full tour guide mode, sharing tidbits of fun facts and snippets of Savannah's history, slowing when they reached points of interest, many of which Carlita already knew about but were more for the benefit of family who were visiting.

"We've reached our first stop." Reese expertly steered the trolley alongside the curb and shifted into park. "Bon appétit, my friends."

Carlita waited until the others got off. "Can't you come with us?"

"There's plenty of room," Pete chimed in. "We would love to have you join us."

"Unfortunately, I can't leave the trolley unattended."

"What a shame. I feel guilty for having you work while we have fun."

"This is fun," Reese insisted. "I love my job, and being with friends makes it even better."

"Perhaps we can make it up to you." Pete grasped his wife's hand and led her toward the steps. "What would you like from the restaurant?"

"I love The Exchange's fried green tomatoes with remoulade."

"You got it."

"Fried green tomatoes," Carlita repeated. "As long as I've lived here, I can't recall if I ever tried one."

"The tomatoes are the restaurant's signature appetizer," Pete said. "We need to get out more."

"You're right. I think we do."

As soon as the others exited, their host ushered them toward River Street, down the steps, and to the restaurant. Although bustling and busy, the hostess sprang into action, leading the large group to their reserved table, offering a picture-perfect view of the Savannah River.

A slew of servers arrived, pouring drinks and placing platters of appetizers on the table. The food included chicken fingers and French fries for the kids, while there were more unique and upscale dishes for the adults.

While they savored and sampled, Sam shared some interesting tidbits about the building, a former cotton warehouse.

"Look Nonna!" PJ pointed excitedly. "I see a big boat out in the water."

Carlita craned her neck, peering out the window. "Good eye, PJ. A large cargo ship is going by. Can you see the men on the deck? They're waving."

He waved both hands in the air. "They can see me."

Gina smoothed her son's hair. "They can see you all the way past the other people walking by and inside the restaurant?" she teased.

"I'm going to be captain of a ship someday," the boy announced. "And ride on even bigger ships."

"Grandpa Pete can teach you everything he knows about sailing the high seas," Carlita said.

"I sure will. In fact, we'll take the Flying Gunner out before you go home. You can guide us along the river."

"I'll be the captain?" Little Paulie became so excited, he literally fell out of his chair and onto the floor.

Pete quickly scooped him up. "Are you okay?"

"Yeah. Can we go now?"

"Not today, but soon." Pete caught his wife's eye over the top of the boy's head and winked. His love for the sea was rubbing off on his young grandson, and it warmed Carlita's heart to hear the excitement in his voice.

"Have you tried a fried green tomato?" Pete slid the dish toward her.

"Not yet." Using her fork, Carlita stabbed the crispy tomato and slid it onto her plate. She poured a dash of sauce on the side, sawed off a piece and dipped it in the remoulade before nibbling the edge. "It's crunchy and tart with…" She struggled to describe the dish.

"A little kick," Pete said.

"Yes. Tart and spicy with a creaminess to it." Carlita polished off the rest of the slice. "It's delicious. No wonder they're Reese's favorite."

The group ate every single bite of food. Pete paid the bill, grabbed the to-go container, and off they went.

Reese, who must've been on the lookout for them, scrambled out of her seat and picked up her microphone. "All aboard!"

Violet broke free and ran ahead of the others. "Can I say something?"

"Sure." Reese handed the microphone to her.

"Mine was yummy in my tummy."

Not to be left out, Gracie, Noel, and PJ took turns making announcements. Little Vinnie was offered his chance, but he hadn't yet warmed up to Reese. He gave her a pouty look, buried his head in his mother's arm and hid his face.

Carlita pulled the schedule Pete had given them from her pocket to check out the next stop, the Oak Tap House, a Colonial-style mansion only a few blocks away. As soon as they arrived, Reese pulled off the street and hit the brakes.

Pete and Carlita, the first to exit, stepped onto the sidewalk to wait for their family and friends to assemble.

Reese tapped her horn and lifted her container of food. "Take your time. I'll be here savoring this delicious treat."

"I hope you enjoy every bite."

"You know it. Thank you. I can't wait to dig in."

"Would you care for a special dish from the Oak Tap House?"

"I..." Reese hesitated.

"What would you like?" Carlita asked. "We feel bad you aren't able to go with us. The least we can do is feed you."

"If you don't mind, their fried pork chops are to die for."

"You got it. In fact, the pork chops are what I planned to order." Pete promised to bring food back before following the others inside the restaurant.

Once again, the staff was expecting them. The hostess led them down the stairs and into the basement, an area of the restaurant which had been converted into a pub and bar.

Seating them off to the side, Carlita noticed a trio of musicians playing classical music in the background. "This is a cool place."

"With an interesting history," Sam said.

"We certainly lucked out. Not only do we have Reese as a tour guide, but we have Savannah's best to tell us all about these historic places," Carlita said. "Feel free to share, although we don't want you to think we're putting you to work during your time off."

"Not at all," Sam said. "I'm happy to be here."

Mercedes scooched closer to him. "This place is giving off a creepy kind of vibe."

"It's rumored to be haunted by the owner who built it. He made his mark in the cotton industry. He, along with a few others."

Brittney shivered involuntarily. "Hopefully, the ghosts stay away until we're gone."

A friendly server arrived to introduce herself and her assistant. Because they were ordering entrées, the staff brought out an array of food, all prepared for sharing.

Carlita sampled a piece of Pete's massive fried pork chop, along with sauteed shrimp and scallops. She took a few bites of the side dishes before calling it quits, reminding herself they were making at least two more stops before they had dessert.

The dishes made their rounds with the group oohing and aahing over the selection.

Pete leaned in and whispered in his wife's ear. "I think everyone is enjoying themselves."

"This is a huge hit. Everything I've tasted has been delicious. It's so much fun visiting places I've only heard about. I'm almost ashamed to say I've lived in Savannah for years and never been to any of these restaurants."

"It's time for us to venture out more often, even if it's just the two of us." Pete lifted his glass of sweet tea. "A toast."

Carlita lifted her tea. "A toast."

"To more adventures and less stress."

"Here. Here." They clinked glasses and took a sip. "I haven't had a relaxing day like this in a long time."

"You've even forgotten about the burglars and catching the bad guys," Pete teased.

"Momentarily." Carlita glanced at her watch. "Which reminds me, Autumn should be catching up with us soon."

"She promised to meet us at our next stop."

With the food finished and the children growing restless, they stayed long enough for the server to snap a group photo before they headed out.

Pete was the last to board the trolley. He greeted Reese and placed the container of food on the dashboard. "You might be taking some leftovers home," he warned.

"Leftovers?" Reese popped the top, letting out a gasp when she saw how massive the pork chop was. "Good gravy."

"Yes, I believe there are mashed potatoes and gravy buried beneath the pork chop," Pete joked.

"I'm talking about the size." She balanced the container in her hand. "I won't have to cook for a week."

"It's delicious. I hope you enjoy every bite." Carlita gave her a quick hug. "You're the best trolley guide in Savannah. Thanks again for agreeing to drive us around."

"I'm having a ball," Reese insisted. "This isn't work. It's fun."

As soon as everyone took their seats, they set off for the next stop, where they found Autumn was already there waiting. She greeted Vinnie, Brittney, little Vin, and then Paulie and his tribe. "The whole Garlucci clan is here."

"Because of Pete," Carlita said. "How did the rest of your day go?"

"Slow." Autumn tipped her hand back and forth. "My boss let me leave a few minutes early. What did I miss?"

"Scrumptious dishes, but there's more to come." Pete took a step back, eyeballing the pub, which had previously been used as a movie theater. "I saved the best for you, Autumn."

"Thanks. I've always wanted to check this place out."

"Now's your chance," he said.

Carlita tapped her shoulder. "How did the editing go for the Sterling interview?"

"Not good." Autumn told her Wes had issues. "We lost part of the sound. We'll have to tape the segment again, if Sterling is agreeable. He might not want to be bothered, although it is free publicity. To be honest, I've never met anyone who complained about us having to come back and re-record."

"Tape the segment again?" Carlita's scalp tingled. "That's great news."

Dernice eased in next to her. "The fingerprint from the compact didn't match."

"Murphy's Law," Autumn said. "My gut told me we needed the other daughter's prints."

"I hate to ask, but do you mind contacting Sterling to go back out there seeing how you have a legitimate reason?" Carlita asked.

"Of course not. I'll also mention his daughters again." Autumn tugged on a stray strand of hair.

"We'll have to come up with a clever way to get Tracy's prints."

"The sooner, the better." Carlita had received a disturbing call from her insurance agent, mentioning the vandalism and burglary, and wondering if she planned to file a claim. When questioned, Tony admitted to phoning the agent after finding out that repairing the damaged drainpipe might not be as easy as he first thought.

But when Carlita mentioned the anonymous tipster and insurance fraud, he agreed they should pay for the expense out-of-pocket.

The more she thought about it, the angrier she became. If the Sterlings were behind the burglaries, she wanted them caught and to pay for the damage—not only hers, but Elvira's and Ken Colby's too.

"I'll give him a quick call." Autumn stepped off to the side, returning moments later. "I left a message."

"Shall we go inside?" Pete held the door for the others. "I hope you're still hungry."

Carlita patted her stomach. "I have to admit all the delicious food is starting to hit bottom, but this is a unique eatery, and I can't wait to check it out."

Stepping across the threshold was like stepping into an equal mix of eclectic, modern, and retro. Like all the other stops, the staff was expecting them.

Having reached the official "happy hour," the men ordered craft beers and the women something a little more interesting.

Carlita switched over from all sweet tea to half and half—half sweet and half unsweet. Dishes of food arrived—burgers, onion rings, salads for Shelby and Brittney. Pete seemed eager to order for his wife, and she quickly agreed, knowing she would love whatever he picked.

Her food arrived, and she tried to hide her disappointment at the hamburger the server set in front of her. On closer inspection, she realized it was anything but. Carlita lifted the bun, revealing a golden, crunchy topping. "What is this?"

"A macaroni and cheeseburger."

"I've never seen such a thing," she said. "Fried macaroni and cheese to boot."

"I've had the burger before. It's a real treat."

Carlita cut it in half and took a big bite. The crunchy coating complimented the cheesy goodness. The hamburger itself was perfectly prepared. She closed her eyes, letting out a sigh of pure delight. "This is the best burger I've ever tasted."

"I knew you would like it." Pete bit into his. "It's as good as I remember."

While they ate, Sam told them about the restaurant's history and shared a story about having visited not long after moving to Savannah.

By the time Carlita finished her first half, she called it quits and asked for a box to take the leftovers home.

She felt a tap on her shoulder. Autumn, with a grim expression on her face, stood behind her. "Hey, Autumn. Is there a problem with your food?"

"No. It's delish. Thank you for inviting me. It's about the other."

"Russell Sterling?"

"He returned my call. He isn't interested in having us come back to re-record the segment."

"Great." Carlita's heart sank. "It looks like we're at a standstill, unless we can figure out some other way to get Tracy Sterling's fingerprints."

Chapter 27

The evening ended with ice cream and sodas at the iconic Leopold's Ice Cream shop. Afterward, friends and family gathered at Pete and Carlita's place with coffee for the adults and board games, hosted by Violet, for the children.

Dernice was the first to bring up the burglaries and their current dilemma of not having a match. "I know Lindsay and Tracy both work full time at the dealership. There has to be a way to get a set of Tracy's fingerprints."

"Short of waltzing in there and demanding she give them to us, I'm fresh out of ideas," Carlita said.

"Wait a minute." Dernice tapped the side of her forehead. "I completely forgot."

"Forgot about what?"

"Friday is donut dash day. El cheapo Sterling springs for donuts every Friday morning for the office staff," she explained.

"How will buying donuts help us?"

"Tracy never missed a donut day. In fact, because she's the gal Friday, she's in charge of picking up the donuts. She takes her father's fancy luxury SUV to the Donuts on Main donut shop every Friday morning like clockwork. All I gotta do is get my buddy, Frankie, to offer her a free latte to sip while she's waiting for her order, and voila! We have our prints."

"With our luck, Tracy will call in sick and someone else will pick up the donuts," Carlita muttered.

"Not a chance. I offered to go while I was working there incognito. I thought Tracy was gonna have a meltdown. As soon as I get home, I'll get on the horn with Frankie to see if he's working in the morning."

Luigi was the first to leave. Dernice left not long after. Shelby, Tony, and their girls were next. Mercedes, Autumn and Sam weren't far behind, having already made plans to meet up with friends in the City Market.

All that was left was Paulie, Vinnie, and their families, along with Pete and Carlita.
"I know you're gung-ho to nab the burglars, but at least nobody died," Vinnie said.

"True. I suppose I could let it go. The Sterlings aren't hardened criminals." Carlita pursed her lips. "It's not even the fact it happened. I guess it's the principle of the matter."

"Because the father is covering for his daughters," Pete said.

"Yep. If more people cared about doing the right thing, even if it means punishing your children for doing wrong, there would be less trouble in the world."

"I admire your determination, Ma." Vinnie squeezed her hand. "It's a good thing you aren't working up in Jersey with me. You would have a field day catching customers who do some...questionable things in the casino."

"I'm sure I would."

Long after the evening ended and Carlita and Pete turned in, she found herself wide awake and staring at the ceiling. Perhaps she should let it go despite the fact Russell Sterling wasn't doing his daughters any favors by letting their behavior not only slide, but covering for them.

Even if they could prove Tracy Sterling was the person who broke into Elvira's building—and hers—something told her Sterling would do everything in his power to bail her out.

*****

Dernice called Carlita early the next morning. "Frankie's working. I'm gonna swing by there and hide out to collect the evidence."

315

"Do you mind if I tag along?"

"Of course not. I'm hopping into Elvira's car as we speak."

"Elvira's car?"

"I can't very well take the van with EC Security Services plastered all over the side."

"True. Good point."

"I'll swing by and pick you up."

Carlita told her she would be waiting in the parking lot. She threw on some clothes, grabbed a jacket and her purse, and headed out. Because Fridays were typically busy with the pirate ship bookings for weekend events, Pete had already left the house.

With Rambo by her side, they trekked to the sidewalk. As promised, Dernice pulled up within minutes. Carlita opened the door. "Is it okay if Rambo goes with us?"

"Sure. Just don't tell Elvira."

"Not a peep." Carlita ushered her pup into the back before hopping in. "I hope this works out, and this chick shows up for her weekly donut run."

"She will. I'll bet you fifty bucks she'll be at the donut shop between eight thirty and nine."

Cutting across town, they arrived at the small donut shop, a place Carlita had never noticed before, around quarter after eight. Stepping inside, they were greeted by a man, in his late twenties if Carlita had to guess, with dark curly hair and a scruffy beard.

The tantalizing aroma of cinnamon and freshly brewed coffee reminded Carlita she hadn't had her morning fix.

"It smells good in here, Frankie."

"Thanks. You want a cup?"

"We'll take two." Carlita pulled her credit card from her wallet, eyeing the glazed donuts in the display case. "Those look yummy."

"They're my best seller. You wanna try one?"

"Make it two, to go with the coffee."

Frankie poured the coffees and set those, along with the donuts, on the counter before ringing up the purchase. "You gave me a brief rundown last night, but remind me of the game plan."

"It's simple. When Tracy Sterling gets here for her Friday morning donut run, hand her a cup of coffee. Not a to-go one, but a ceramic mug. We need her fingerprints."

"She doesn't drink hot coffee. Tracy is more of an iced coffee drinker."

"Then serve her iced coffee in a glass," Dernice said. "Maybe entice her by telling her you have something new for her to try."

"For free. She's cheap."

"The apple doesn't fall far from the tree," Carlita said.

"Good idea." Frankie gave them a thumbs up. "I can do it."

"Let's go hide in the kitchen." Dernice lifted the counter bar separating the employee area and led Carlita and her pup into the back.

Not a minute later, the overhead bell chimed. Carlita couldn't resist. She peeked out the pass-thru to see who it was. A teenager stood at the counter, chatting with Frankie, who was fixing a cold-brew coffee and bagging a croissant.

The teen left, and it grew quiet. Long moments dragged by. Five. Ten.

Carlita started to pace, anxiously eyeing the clock. Half an hour had passed. Customers came and went. "Maybe she won't show."

"She'll show."

The bell chimed again.

Dernice tiptoed to the window. She quickly ducked down, silently mouthing the words, "she's here."

Frankie greeted the customer. A conversation ensued. Unfortunately, she and Dernice were too far away. Carlita couldn't hear what was being said. The back and forth went on for several minutes. The bell chimed again and then it grew quiet.

Frankie appeared in the doorway. "The coast is clear. You can come out now. She's gone."

"Did you get the fingerprints?"

He held up a glass with a napkin wrapped around the bottom. "Was there ever any doubt? Am I good or what?"

"No, Frankie. You're not good." Dernice whistled loudly and gave him a hearty slap on the back. "You're great. Now, all I need to do is get this thing over to the lab."

Chapter 28

"Do you have to leave so soon?" Carlita hugged Vinnie tightly, reluctantly releasing her grip. "It seems like you just got here."

"I'm sorry, Ma. We gotta get back to Jersey." Vinnie picked up his small son, who stood tugging on his pant leg. "The good news is you get to look forward to the Garlucci-Taylor family road trip to Jersey."

"Which isn't too far off," Brittney said. "I've already reserved suites at the casino's hotel, enough rooms for everyone. It'll be fun."

"Even with Elvira there?" Carlita arched her eyebrow. "I hope you know what you're getting yourselves into."

"Into a fun family adventure," Paulie joked. "I wonder what sort of trouble we'll find."

"Not too much." Carlita playfully wagged her finger at her children. "No mafia hits, illegal activity, or bodies popping up."

"Or burglaries taking place," Tony interrupted.

"Speaking of burglaries, what happened to Lindsay and Tracy Sterling?" Paisley asked.

"The investigators were able to match the fingerprint found on Elvira's ductwork to Tracy Sterling's fingerprint from the donut shop's glass."

Mercedes picked up. "When questioned, Russell Sterling admitted he had hired EC Investigative Services to find out why his business was coming up short and missing money. Dernice, who was working undercover, had been able to tie some of the transactions to specific employee identification numbers."

"And when exactly did Sterling find out about the investigation's findings?" Pete wondered aloud.

"The day before Elvira left for Alaska. She submitted her report with proof of the siphoned funds and links to the employee accounts."

"Which, thanks to Dernice getting permission to use Elvira's handy dandy backdoor system for tracking down almost any company information, we discovered those ID numbers belong to Sterling's daughters, who were employed by Sterling Automotive Group."

"With one of them being in charge of financing." Dernice rubbed her fingers together. "Lindsay Sterling had the perfect position to steal...from her own father, no less."

"To make it look a little more random, they also vandalized the pawn shop and broke into Colby's Corner Store. Meanwhile, the real goal was to break into Elvira's office and steal the report," Mercedes said. "Although some of them were electronic files, which meant they would have had to crack into her online filing system to locate the information."

Dernice shook her head. "I have to say they were two of the most bumbling burglars I've ever seen."

"I don't think they put a lot of thought into it," Steve said. "I remember talking to Sterling at the fundraiser. He was with a young woman. Next thing I know, they took off."

"Because the daughter was only there to make sure the coast was clear to start burglarizing our businesses," Carlita said. "The cat burglar, the one who did the actual breaking in was Tracy, the more athletic sibling."

"She's a former gymnast who started working for her father after she took a hard fall and was forced to quit competing," Dernice explained. "I found that little tidbit of information online yesterday."

"I'm guessing when Pete and I showed up on Russell Sterling's doorstep, telling him about the burglaries, he put two and two together and realized it was his daughters," Carlita said.

"You're absolutely correct," Sam said. "I learned from my buddy down at the precinct that Sterling confessed he'd planned to confront his daughters about the missing money and break-in at his place. Before he was able to, Lindsay and Tracy discovered their father had hired Elvira's firm. They were afraid they were about to be found out and decided to steal her records."

"Not knowing it was already too late," Dernice said. "Officer Jonkers went over to Sterling's place after finding out there might be a connection. He didn't want to see them end up in jail, so he lied to her about his incident to cover for his kids."

"Which makes him an accessory to a crime," Sam said.

"I'm curious about the piece of fabric we found inside the air vent," Carlita said.

"It was a big fat nothing burger," Dernice said. "Lindsay and Tracy are insisting it didn't belong to them, although I have my doubts. There's no way to link it which means I wasted my time crawling in there to collect potential evidence."

"What do you think will happen to them—all three of them?" Mercedes asked.

Sam shrugged. "First offense with no previous records? Most likely a slap on the wrist, especially if Elvira, Ken Colby and Carlita don't press charges."

Dernice gave them two thumbs down. "Elvira might not be on board to let it slide. Every time I talk to her, she's complaining about the cost of repairing the ductwork."

"I'm sure Mr. Sterling and she can work out an arrangement," Carlita said.

"Even if he doesn't, I have this." Dernice triumphantly waved a piece of paper in the air. "I'll have the extra cash-ola to pay for the repairs. Elvira has a prime project she wants me to take on. We cut a deal, and she's agreed to cover the ductwork repair."

Tony tapped his mother's shoulder. "What about you, Ma? Are you going to press charges?"

Carlita thought about it, how she would feel if she were in Russell Sterling's shoes. Although she knew very little about his daughters, reading between the lines, they were indulged, spoiled and entitled children. If he continued to cover for them, to excuse their behavior and not allow them to learn from their mistakes, something told her history would repeat itself.

In other words, Sterling would get what he deserved. "We all make mistakes. Something tells me they won't return to Walton Square. Besides, they didn't do anything other than break my window and damage a drainpipe. I'm not sure what Ken plans to do. That's entirely up to him." Carlita cast a glance toward the door. "Autumn should be here any minute. She said she was right around the corner and had an update on the case. Some sort of breaking news."

The pawn shop's front door flew open. Autumn appeared. "Sorry if I kept you waiting."

"No worries. We were just talking about the Sterlings, wondering what would happen to them."

"Wonder no more. The father and daughters are in hot water." Autumn pulled her cell phone from her pocket. "Channel Eleven got a hot tip about breaking news at Sterling's dealership. Wes was the cameraman on scene and just sent me some footage you gotta see."

"We can watch it right here." Tony grabbed a remote and turned the nearby television on.

Autumn forwarded the recording and he cast it to the screen. Everyone grew quiet as Sterling Automotive Group's building popped up. One of the station's reporters appeared, claiming a prominent local businessman was being taken into custody for threatening investigators who were there to question his daughters.

"We were told by bystanders there was some sort of standoff and now we're waiting to see what happens." The reporter continued to talk. She abruptly stopped and shifted to the side. "I believe the authorities are exiting the building now."

The camera zoomed in on the front door. A flurry of officers emerged. In their midst was a handcuffed Russell Sterling, his head down as he was escorted from the building. Walking only steps behind them were Lindsay and Tracy Sterling, their faces red and appearing visibly shaken.

Carlita watched as the trio were placed inside patrol cars. The cars left and the camera returned to the reporter. "We've been told this may be linked to a recent string of burglaries in the Walton Square area. We will update you as soon as we get more information."

The screen switched to a commercial and Tony turned the television off. "Well...I guess we know the women aren't going to get away with it after all."

Steve clapped his hands. "Justice is, or will be, served. I feel much better now."

"Because the good deeds of our neighbors didn't backfire and we don't have to worry about thugs breaking in and stealing from us?"

"Yep. Paisley and I are now caught up on our mortgage, have some emergency funds set aside, and bookings are on the rise. Not only did the fundraiser bring in money, but helped rustle up new customers."

"We have several first time clients booked out for the next month," Paisley beamed.

"I love it when a plan comes together." Carlita pressed her hand to her chest. "Friends helping friends. It's what Walton Square and Savannah are all about."

The end.

Dear Reader,

*I hope you enjoyed reading, "Bungled Burglaries."
Would you please take a moment to leave a
review? It would mean so much. Thank you! -
Hope Callaghan*

More Made in Savannah Mysteries Coming Soon!

Join The Fun

Get Updates On New Releases, FREE and Discounted eBooks, Giveaways, & More!

hopecallaghan.com

Read More by Hope

Made in Savannah Cozy Mystery Series

After the mysterious death of her mafia "made man" husband, Carlita Garlucci makes a shocking discovery. Follow the Garlucci family saga as Carlita and her daughter try to escape their NY mob ties and make a fresh start in Savannah, Georgia. They soon realize you can run but can't hide from your past.

Cruise Director Millie Mystery Series

Cruise Director Millie Mystery Series is the new spin-off series from the wildly popular Millie's Cruise Ship Cozy Mysteries.

Millie's Cruise Ship Cozy Mystery Series

Hoping for a fresh start after her recent divorce, sixty something Millie Sanders, lands her dream job as the assistant cruise director onboard the "Siren of the Seas." Too bad no one told her murder is on the itinerary.

333

Easton Island Mystery Series

Easton Island is the continuing saga of one woman's journey from incredible loss to finding a past she knew nothing about, including a family who both embraces and fears her and a charming island that draws her in. This inspirational women's fiction series is for lovers of family sagas, friendship, mysteries, and clean romance.

Lack of Luxury Series (Liz and the Garden Girls)

Green Acres meets the Golden Girls in this brand new cozy mystery spin-off series featuring Liz and the Garden Girls!

Garden Girls Cozy Mystery Series

A lonely widow finds new purpose for her life when she and her senior friends help solve a murder in their small Midwestern town.

Garden Girls - The Golden Years

The brand new spin-off series of the Garden Girls Mystery series! You'll enjoy the same fun-loving characters as they solve mysteries in the cozy town of Belhaven. Each book will focus on one of the Garden Girls as they enter their "golden years."

Divine Cozy Mystery Series

After relocating to the tiny town of Divine, Kansas, strange and mysterious things begin to happen to businesswoman, Jo Pepperdine and those around her.

Samantha Rite Mystery Series

Heartbroken after her recent divorce, a single mother is persuaded to book a cruise and soon finds herself caught in the middle of a deadly adventure. Will she make it out alive?

Sweet Southern Sleuths Short Stories Series

Twin sisters with completely opposite personalities become amateur sleuths when a dead body is discovered in their recently inherited home in Misery, Mississippi.

Meet Hope Callaghan

Hope Callaghan is an American mystery author who loves to write clean, fun-filled women's fiction mysteries with a touch of faith and romance. She is the author of more than 100 novels in ten different series.

Born and raised in a small town in West Michigan, she now lives in Florida with her husband. She is the proud mother of 3 wonderful children.

When she's not doing the thing she loves best - writing mysteries - she enjoys cooking, traveling and reading books.

Get a free cozy mystery book, new release alerts, and giveaways at <u>hopecallaghan.com</u>

Smoky Pasta Burrata Recipe

Ingredients:

1 cup walnuts

3/4 cup Italian bread crumbs

16 oz jar of whole roasted red peppers

Zest and juice of 1 lemon

2 garlic cloves, peeled and quartered

1 tsp. crushed red pepper flakes, divided

½ cup plus 2 Tbsp. extra-virgin olive oil

Kosher salt

2 tsp. smoked paprika

12 oz. box of spiral pasta

1 lb. mixed ripe tomatoes, cut into bite-size pieces (about 3 cups)

4 oz. Parmesan, shredded or finely chopped

1 cup basil leaves, torn if large

Directions:

-Preheat oven to 350°.

-Toast walnuts on a rimmed baking sheet, tossing halfway through, until golden brown, up to 12 minutes.

-Remove from oven. Set aside and let cool.

-Puree roasted red peppers, lemon juice, garlic, ½ tsp. red pepper flakes, and about one-quarter of the cooled walnuts in food processor until smooth.

-While still mixing, gradually add ½ cup oil.

-Blend until thick.

-Season with salt, to taste.

-Cook pasta in a large pot of boiling salted water, stirring occasionally, until al dente.

-Drain and rinse under cold water

-In large bowl, toss cooked pasta with half of the romesco (red pepper mixture) to coat. Set aside.

-Finely chop the remaining toasted walnuts.

-Heat 2 Tbsp. oil in a medium saucepan over medium heat.

-Cook while continuously stirring the breadcrumbs, lemon zest, smoked paprika and remaining ½ tsp. red pepper flakes until the breadcrumbs are golden brown, 3-5 minutes. (watch closely because they will easily burn.)

-Remove from heat.

-Toss pasta with remaining romesco dressing.

-Fold in bite-size tomatoes, Parmesan, and the rest of the walnuts.

-Sprinkle breadcrumb mixture over pasta.

-Top with basil.

-Serve with a side salad and garlic bread.

Made in the USA
Columbia, SC
02 May 2025

57474246R00207